A Guide to Meditation

First published 2016

The body needs to be free of emotion,

The mind needs be still,

This is not normal, but it is natural,

This book is to help bring this about

Meditativeness begins when the body is Relaxed,

The pressure to think is proportional to the discomfort in the body,

The discomfort in the body is emotion from the past, or in the present moment

The thoughts that you have are a reflection of the emotion in the Body if you have anxiety in the body your thoughts will be those of fear.

The Beginning of meditation

The beginning stages of meditation looking
At some fundamentals,what is meditation, why meditate,
how long, what you can expect, what is helpful to read,and the
actual experience of it.

The middle stage of meditation

we will look in more detail at the problems involved with moving
into the body, using a
few more tools, changing your perception lose more
emotion/tightness become more still, we look at how when we
help ouselves we also help the
animals around us with our understanding of energy and emotion

The later stage of meditation

we look at the energy in the body, the emotion and stillness the
energy centres
  our perceptions of what we think we are
  we move into the subtleties of ego

This book is about 36 years of meditation and experience as a
healer , up to todays understanding , its about how to empty the
body of emotion ,emotion which leads to illness and dis-ease and a
noisy
mind ,about bringing it to life , about stilling the mind,
About being present , master of your own body.

I guess before I start I need to talk about the writing of it,the book
that is, I have tried many times to write a book and many times
failed or I suppose it would probably be better to I say to that I
have learnt a

lot of valuable lessons about writing , how I find it so utterly
impossible sometimes, so I will say before I start that I find i
cannot be confined to chapters and segments easily and going over
and

over improving it because when I do that I lose the initial
essence so I have to jump off a cliff and just do it, i apologise to
you for the fact that it will not always read easily sometimes I will
have to find a way and speed at which I can just sit and speak into
the now marvellous modern voice recognition software that is
available that has at least made it possible for me to ramble on,
when I do a talk or a course, I often say that I'm like an old David
Brown tractor , a little bit slow to get started but eventually I chug
into life and once im off and running im ok for the rest of the day
but I must admit talking in front of people is actually easier
for me anyway, than writing a book I,m   one of those people that
finds even writing a Christmas card   takes an hour and
then it still comes out naff sometimes my partner says to me what
shall I say on so-and-so,s card I must admit I haven't got a single
clue I find that the experience that I have comes from the belly and
not from the head and so it is very difficult to put feeling and
experiences into words because there seems such a distance between
the belly and the head, I remember quite a few years ago when I was
attempting to write a book and in those days there was no voice
recognition software and I believe I was trying to do it with pen, I
became quite annoyed and despaired at my inability to sprout forth
and a little while later I opened up a book written by osho who in
those days was called bhagwan shree Rajneesh someone asked him
the question, your words seemed to come so easily how do you do it

basically the gist of his answer was that he found it very
difficult indeed to use every single word correctly as every single
word has a
different meaning and it was very difficult for him this made
me feel a lot better, when we read books we are so used to them
being written
in a certain way a certain format to some extent quite sterilised I
remember when I was first setting out in 1978 reading books by a
master called gurdjieff the books 3 of them were called beelzebubs
tales to his grandson they were to put it mildly difficult to read I
persevered for many months but eventually gave up even though all
three cost me about $20 which was a lot in those days, my book will
be nowhere near as difficult to read I hope but some people find
that because I'm an air sign I sometimes flit from one thing to
another quite quickly and they don't know what the heck I'm talking
about but I find that if I just talk naturally then the book will be
closer to the real essence rather than some pasteurised version also
at this point

**it is important that you understand that when you open a
book and place your attention on that book you are placing
your attention on the person who spoke the words and you
will experience there being**

hence masters say that it is the gaps between the words that are important not the words themselves this is what they mean I will at some point reiterate this as it is a very important point, it is an understanding a movement from being a fundamentally mind oriented, word oriented person to a feeling energetic person i.ll tell a story here to describes this many years ago when I was running a vegan bed and breakfast with my then partner we had a chap came along who had lived at the commune in the pune with osho and he stayed with us for a while and when he left he gave me some tapes and some magazines and at the time I was very busy and in the lunch breaks I would come and sit by the window in my chair and each lunchbreak I would go into the most profound ego less state absolutely blissed out for my whole lunch break this was the effect of the energy from the tape and magazine's that were on the window sill on another occasion I bought a Barry long tape called how to stop thinking and placed it into the tape player but before I had turned the player on I noticed that my consciousness had changed in a strong way so I sat back in the chair and watched and it was different from the osho experience in that I felt and I can only describe it as this, that I would be totally bonkers to think, why would I be that crazy, I was absolutely still absolutely silent totally surefooted utterly utterly silent and this was the effect of the tape placing my attention on the tape,

I have had other similar experiences besides these so I will ramble somewhat especially in the early stages of the book telling stories because I find that this is the best way to put my message across and assist understanding

You need to be aware that stillness goes hand in hand with understanding the deeper the understanding the deeper the stillness.

Understanding follows confusion
The deeper your confusion the deeper the
understanding that follows.

Before we begin to look at meditation we need to summarize the body as it is in a normal person and where we are going

So firstly the mind,the reason I am starting the book this way is to outline in plain simple terms the human condition, you will disagree or dislike some of the following but it seems clear to me that unless we know where we are and where we need to head things will be to woolly, meditation is an absolute bugger to understand and so I want to be as clear as I can upfront, the mind as it stands is utterly out of control, it runs non stop 24/7 night and day with no one at the helm if this were a laptop or mobile then it would run out of energy in no time and would be no use whatsoever to the user yet we have become so used to this situation it is classed as the norm(at this point some will say actually your wrong my mind is quiet a lot of the time ,please check this out it is only that you are unaware of the seriousness of the situation) furthermore the mind itself in our society relies soley on external information and we call this knowledge and are proud of it and prize it above all else, and confuse

It with intelligence which it most definitely is not, in fact knowledge has a deadening effect the more of it we store the less intelligence can make its way through, intelligence is there in the moment if the mind is still and empty it is part and parcel of the energy that we are, on top of this because the mind is a nonstop out of control machine it has taken on the role of self, in other words it conceives itself to be the the person,this is called ego, when in fact its rightful place is just a tool of the body, not in charge of it,

So what is required of the mind to bring it back to its rightful harmonious place, it needs to be still,and empty, free of conceptions, still until needed, a little knowledge but not enough to be a burden, in being empty intelligence is readily and instantly available when needed, and ego is no longer a problem because the mind has its rightful place as part of a balanced being

The body

So now lets look at the body of normal man, it is in tension from head to toe, and right to the centre, this tension is the direct result of the emotion that we collect and store unconsciously everyday and as we get older the body builds up more

so we get illness,s such as arthritis, etc,etc, this
emotion in the body goes hand in glove with the noise in
the mind so if you have anger in the body you will have
angry thoughts, and vice versa all this emotion leads to a
constant unconcious discomfort which creates a
pressure to think, so imagine if there is no emotion
stored, and the body is empty then so will the mind and
that in a nutshell is the message of the book empty out
the body keep it free of the emotion that builds up daily,
and meditaition is achievable and natural, illness will
fall away and energy will change as will the ego as stillness
is practised in longer doses, practiced in the beginning
eventually becoming the natural alert state of a master

The early stage of meditation

so again let me reiterate turn your attention within and
check yourself out
we will be looking at this checking yourself out situation in
the pages to
come it is exactly the same process as if you have a client,
patient in front of you that you wish to help, whether it be

So that you can read their body to assist with the problem, being attentive to your body first is essential so as to know whats yours and whats theres

this

is the way I work and have done for the last 25 odd years more on this later so let's get back to where we were I'm probably doing an aquarian thingy jumping about so let's get back to the beginning, the early stages for me back in 1978 I found a book shop in Brisbane that was solely a spiritual bookshop that was filled to the roof with all manner of spiritual books and I started where anyone tends to start which is the fairly simple stuff metaphysics formal religion I looked at Christianity buddism Hinduism etc etc etc I was lucky at that stage in my life or maybe it wasn't luck that I was a courier and had many quiet periods throughout the day that allowed me to read and read and read and read on most days I would read for 2 to 3 hours at least and at night and early mornings I would meditate sometimes for 3 to 4 hours at a stretch until tears would roll down my cheeks with pain of sitting cross-legged which I thought in those days was necessary and the obligatory joining the finger and thumb thingy that you do when you see the photos I now know of course that this is just the Western concept of what meditation

Should be like, but of course without the understanding

that as a person who has been brought up using a chair my body is just not capable of sitting comfortably in this position for any length of time so for anyone out there who is just starting out let's take posture as a starting point I must tell you a funny story at this stage the bookshop that I was telling you about I went into this one day and there was a book by Bhagwan shree Rajneesh who later changed his name to osho there was one of his books called

above all don't wobble and I remember that at the time posture was something that was on my mind and I bought this book even though it was expensive because I thought that above all don't wobble was what was required when you were sitting in the cross-legged posture that is how green I was looking back at it I find it hard to believe so coming back to posture sit comfortably in a chair up right so that you don't fall asleep,

in the beginning meditation will be something that you will have as a timed slot in your day but this will expand over time in the same way that an athlete might start with 30 minutes 1 hour and then build his way up to 2 or three hours, a master is meditative (meditativeness is the stillness that comes when meditation has worked) 24 hours a day, lets come back to posture so you sit in Your chair up right feet on the ground by the way and the only reason for this is so that in the beginning you don't fall to sleep you want to become conscious not unconscious so you sit in your chair

back up straight feet on the floor with or without shoes hands rested comfortably now this is a standard posture but I like to throw out the rulebook let me give you an idea of what I'm saying when I lived in australia it was always warm so I would get up at five or six in the morning sit beside my bed and meditate for an hour or two in the morning before going to work when I came back to England I just could not bring myself to get out of bed at that time of day because most of the year it was dark most of the year it was raining I am affected quite badly by the weather

so when I came back to England I was faced with a situation
where I had to change my routine or give up so when I awoke at six or
seven in the morning I would simply stay there in a nice warm bed and
begin meditating likewise when I went to bed I would meditate for an hour
or
two at night this in years to come would be something that I would
prolong and I would meditate all night sometimes for two or three nights a
week in fact nearly always two or three or even four nights a week right
throughout the night so you see meditation is not about rigidity to posture
it's about understanding who you are, what you are not, it's not about
these
surface shallow outer things it's a much deeper part of your being, it is
worth noting here that I had meditaded in Australia enough so that I did
not fall asleep or go into the dream state when I was lying down
which is always the possibility in this position , so now let's move on to
time, how long should you meditate again no hard and fast rule when I
started off literally on the first day I dived straight in to an hour or more
even though I had absolutely no idea whatsoever what meditation was,
for me I read the word and it was like being hit over the head I just had
to do it and the only thing I knew was cross-legged fingers thingy close
your eyes and see what happened this would be sometimes two or three
hours and I learned as I went along very slowly in the beginning , so you
are comfortable with 10
mins great 20 mins great again there are no great rules you decide you
may have a burning   passion inside as I did that you need to satisfy this
also applies to the reading of books in the early stages you may find that
like me you need to read and read and read and no matter how much you
read it will not satisfy you just want to know more and that's great that's
how it should be, in the early stage you read a lot then you go through a
phase where you don't wish to read at all, then you may settle at a happy
medium just read a chapter or two a day I find that reading is so utterly
utterly mundane compared to the real experience that can be found

inside,that I read only a chapter or two if im on holiday , let me say at this point that for those of you who are about to become meditators or are meditators in the early stages meditaition is difficult and frustrating utterly confusing

absolutely no fun at all you just keep going because you know you must your drawn to it like a moth to a flame , what I hope this book will do is quickly get you through this initial stage so that you can move onto the the more finer stages were you begin to understand and move forward

in the early stages you may assume meditation to be in fact, it's highly likely that you will assume, that meditation is something that will give you an altered state of consciousness if you are really lucky and you are doing something right or that you should feel relaxed so let's look at what meditation is, what is required of it ,what you will be like be for and after when you begin to meditate your body will be filled with emotion your mind will be full of thoughts you will be unconscious of this and you will have no way of ridding yourself of this problem you won't even know That it's a problem and if you are you will assume that everyone has it , it is part of human

existence and it will be a new idea to you that you can live without the body filled with tension aches and pains and that the mind can be still ordinarily you will only be conscious of your body when it is in pain and you would rarely if ever be conscious of the fact that you continuously think twenty four seven so meditation is there to address this issue , and as society becomes faster and faster so this mind body issue becomes more of a problem life becomes faster more to think of , my previous partner was a brilliant psychic and one-day she experienced a past life as a Native American and when I asked what it was like we were surprised that the most striking thing that she noticed was how still she was as she sat on a horse within the native cultures as within all of the older cultures stillness of mind and awareness of body and the belly area an important part of their culture in Western cultures it has never been so ,

So it is a new idea, in a nutshell this is what meditation is all about dissolving the emotion of past events that get trapped in the body and cause mental noise, mental chatter and emotional

disturbance are one and the same. Do you see what I mean you are sitting and you were hoping for an experience you are highly likely to be using a technique may be counting down or listening to a cd where you will be floating over a lily pond or some such thing, you may well go to a a meditation group that is taken by a person who will do what she calls a guided meditation were again she will lead you down a path and you come to a lily pond or you're sitting under a palm tree or some such thing , for me this is not meditation it is more to do with the fact that the person taking the group is a psychic and will ask you after you have done the group what is it that you have you seen, such and such did you see such and such ,oh this was very helpful for you that you experience this again excuse me for being disrespectful but this is not meditation move on leave it behind do not get stuck in this stage of your understanding of meditation you need to understand this point that throughout all of your meditation stages but especially in the early years you will need to be constantly brave enough to drop the phase your in and the technique that you're trying the book that you're reading drop it and move on this doesn't really apply if you follow the golden rule of always read books by Masters always have as your fundamental every day basic reading material a book

by your own chosen master do not spend too much time on books by non Masters of course in the early stages you will want to read and read and read and a master is very deep very profound and you may find that even one chapter will be hard to read, you,ll have a great need to read lots of different books but my suggestion is make your central core books spoken by your master those words will be completely unedited not a single word will have been changed in the making of that book every single word will be important, whereas with other material that you read you can read and read and read, with books by a master just one or two words is

sufficient to be a life changer if you can hear it, so we have covered
posture and time, reading material I can't really give you material because
this is really something that you must be drawn to yourse but I guess I
could give you some Masters that you could at least start with and you
may well find that one of them is for you if we start with Krishnamurti as
reading material to get an idea of the way in which a master sees things, but
Krishnamurti is not someone that I would recommend easily I apologise
to Krishnamurti but even many years later I am still angry with him for not
being more constructive , you have osho who I would suggest is the
most important master of our century, you have Barry long who is a
different character he comes across as much harder much more masculine
he was an Australian and he was a journalist and so comes across as tough
hard but extremely to the point and I could not recommend him enough,
especially his cd,s how to stop thinking I think they still come as a three
pack barry has some really great material, you have Eckhart tolle who is
also very clear,soft and to the point he talks of the pain body, this is really
the four Masters that I have experience of and are of my generation so I
apologise if I am a little out of date with one or two that are around now
one more thing that comes to mind is a of book by
Paramahansa yogannanda called auto biography of Yogi this is a
great book if you are just starting out its paramahansas life story and
the story of his master which began in India and moves to America it's a
great read Pararmahansa himself has a devotional way which was never for
me
and maybe in a modern sophisticated world is becoming less and less I had
a relative who was a Baptist preacher who used to claim his love of God
and give his wife a black eye and they would both arrive at Chapel in
separate vehicles so I was never a great lover of the devotional to
claim your love of God this personified idea of God was to me crazy
so again so I guess it's time to actually move to the actual task of
meditation itself we spoke just now about how you probably see

Meditation as something that will give you a nice experience if you are
lucky, and if you are sitting long enough and if you technique takes
you there, what I have to do now is to somehow put across in words the
essence of meditation and meditativeness so that you understand that
a technique is only a simple early stage(,in a similar way to when you learn
reiki in the beginning you learn how and where to place your hands
but after a while that becomes unnessasary as you will feel confident
enough to place your hands where they are needed most,) if you feel that
you still need a technique then that's fine carry on with it until you feel you
need it no longer,then you will be ready to look at the next stage so for me
the first stage is the same as the last stage, and that is you turn your
attention in and be an observer of what is there, the understanding of the
observer will change and the body will change, and we will dissect this as
we go along, but this is essentially meditation leading to mastery,

the one who is observing is pure awareness and that's what
you are, and what you are observing is what you are not,

and in observing what you are not what is not real it will dissolve , and
you will be left with what you are which is pure awareness, free of all
limited concepts, emotion and ignorance, so as you hear that, you will not
really resonate with it in the same way that you do with a technique, you
see a technique will be enjoyed by the ego a technique will strengthen the
ego a technique is still doing so a technique is very comfortable for you, it
is what you've always done, it is an add on process rather than a taking
away dissolving process so you will be drawn towards technique, please

understand this you will feel discomfort when I tell you that you must just observe be an observer, be a witness as osho calls it, face yourself it is also discomforting and downright painful at times when you face what you have in your body and your mind so please do not allow yourself the luxury of thinking oh this is not for me I prefer another technique, that is your mind fooling you into being busied kept busy with another technique another enjoyable hobby , it is possible for me to be a little to hard on technique we need to look at issues like that of technique in a little more depth before we move on because it is something that you need to understand, if you take a technique such as Vippassna this is a technique that has created more enlightened beings than any other technique so how could I say for instance that there should be no technique, when Poonji (hwl poonja) was asked what technique he would recommend he said absolutely no technique when pressed time after time he still said absolutely no technique but eventually he said do not let a single thought settle in your mind this was his only technique if you ask Krishnamurti or Barry long the same question the answer would be pretty much the same if you ask osho the same question it would be different because osho used every technique in the book and many more besides so is osho wrong and the others right no it is simply that osho understood that eventually all doing all technique must fall away must be given up but to get to that point some people need a technique to take them there and if they push that technique really hard to its limits they'll eventually say dammit I give up and that is when a breakthrough will come also it is a matter of vibration, frequency osho used to say that all of the words that he used all of the techniques that he gave were just to keep you amused whilst his love and energy melted you down left you ego less, the underlying reasoning behind meditation is a taking away process rather than an add-on and a technique really is an add-on rather than a pure taking away a pure meltdown a technique is something that you do, something that you use, something that will keep you amused rather than a taking away process which is the underlying understanding for meditation, when you start out as a healer you may be drawn to reiki for instance and you will be given a technique of where to place your hands, but after a while you will find that you know where your hands should be because you begin to understand what you are doing, so you will move from technique to understanding the technique was useful in the beginning, and this is the way it can be with meditation if you are drawn to a technique that's fine, eventually it will fall away as you understand , so moving on when I suggest that you just be an observer of yourself be alert be attentive to the noise and the emotion within, in the beginning you will still be doing,trying , this is because this is normal in the world and this is what

you're used to, you can,t imagine doing it any other way but after many months or years the one who is struggling and trying hard to observe and is analysing and analytical about the body and the mind and the pain or the illness that you are observing this observer becomes less and less,(because in the beginning you observe as a person) you will

become less analytical, less hopeful, less wanting, less trying ,eventually you are a pure observer a pure witness pure awareness that's all that is left and that is the meditation process, let me give you an analogy if you have a cat looking up at the sky and a weatherman looking up at the sky the cat is just looking empty staring into space but the weatherman is analysing the clouds predicting the future looking at where the clouds came from how they were formed giving them a name being analytical and knowledgeable so if you had a dial in front of you with the weatherman on the right and the cat on the left in the beginning the needle on the dial would be pointing right over to the right towards the weatherman and eventually after many years the dial would be over pointing towards the cat, you would have moved from analytical to just empty being, at this stage you will say I,m not sure I really want that thankyou but that will be the process

In the beginning you want to have an experience you want
enlightenment so you can use a technique to keep focused on yourself for
instance a technique such as vipassna this constantly calls you back to
watching observing the breath and eventually the technique
of observing the breath eventually even that would be too much just too
much too much doing just be an observer, so again let's come back to
being an observer of the inner space you have a slightly better idea now
of understanding of technique and whether you
should have one or not, and either is fine, the way that I am describing
here would be classed as no technique we are not observing the breath or
bringing the attention to the belly or working our way up from the feet etc
but having said that the way in which we will do things has a sort of
routine, I realise that you need some sort of routine that you can stick to
and feel comfortable with as you start so as you look in the beginning the
first thing you will notice is that the feeling in the body is probably
uncomfortable the mind is probably noisy and I say probably it would be
nothing short of a miracle if it were not unless you are a seasoned
meditator and had faced this down in previous sessions so let's come to the
Observing what you do is to look at the
grossest problem first what that means is you start with whatever is giving
you most trouble so it could be that as your sit you have an aching back,
you have a knee that is playing up so you could decide for instance
rather than start with your head you could bring your attention down to
your knee keep your attention there very gently just observe feel it and
feel it just keep your attention there, the idea of this is that this will
dissolve the underlying reason for the problem this in itself really is a
whole chapter and we better deal with this at a later stage because it's just
too big a subject to to deal with here let's just say be aware of it face
it feel it stay with it don't take your attention from it , underlying this
physical pain on the surface of your body underneath is an emotional
causation okay I know what you're thinking so you may have fallen down

And it may have been an accident I had a lady say to me once, I was taking a
group in London and she said that(I had been talking about this chap
who was in the room and had his whole leg in a metal frame) and she said
well what about rusty over there his wasn't an emotional problem and so
we looked at Rusty's problem, Rusty was a hang glider instructor who had
fallen out of the sky from a height of 100 m, yes when you reach the
ground it was a physical problem but up to that point when I asked Rusty
what emotion he felt he said it was the closest to terror that you're ever
likely to know to the thinking logical Western mind the physical is what
you see the physical is what you deal with , it seems somewhat illogical to
think in terms of the feeling the energy the emotion the thought that could
be locked into that area but what you have in a situation like this is that
you have the simple straightforward structural damage and underneath you
have the emotion and the thought locked in as a major factor in slowing
down the healing process you see the emotion is like a cloud like a sludge it
will slow the area right down so that no energy flows and then no blood
flow so you can have a physical problem and without any underlying
mental or emotional problem that physical top layer will heal itself and be
without to much pain quite quickly, let me tell you a short story here
again just to demonstrate what I mean some time ago i managed to break
down the stiffness the final piece of stiffness in my neck and shoulders
That had been there for may many years and when this started to
flow again and became soft and the energy was flowing underneath I had a
toothache on and off for about a week but I realised it wasn't a toothache
of this lifetime but facial damage from another life from another time so I
didn't go to the dentist and it passed this is not the complete story really
about one month prior to this incident I had had a toothache in that back
part of the jaw and had said to the dentist its so painful it's got to be an
abscess can you just remove it so she took an x-ray and said and showed
me the x-ray and said that the tooth is perfect so when it happened again

I knew that the so-
called toothache was no such thing and as well as this I had flashbacks to
the actual event so and and throughout my 30 years as a healer I've come
across this not only in my own body but other bodies too many times to
mention so do not underestimate the ability of emotion and thought
Deep in the body to cause pain and slow down the healing process on the
Surface, ill just give you one more example many years ago I used to sit
with therapists whodidn't really understand what I would call mysticism
which is what we are talking about here this is a mystical path the path of a
therapist is a totally different route I used to sit in this group and they
would talk of the body in a certain way the way in which therapists do with
their knowledge, and I used to keep quiet not say much and they would
talk of things such as arthritis in a physical way talking about chondroitin
etc and for me arthritis for instance was always because of a lack of blood
flow on the surface because of a lack of flow underneath,loss of emotional
flow we have an emotional vascular system in the same as we do an
energetic or blood vascular system but this is mentioned almost nowhere,
the energetic vascular system is of course dealt with with acupuncture, so
coming back to the therapists describing their treatment of arthritis,   many
years later this therapist came over and we were chatting and he didn't
really remember or know that this was my understanding of arthritis but he
said that in the Lancet they had just discovered that the pain of arthritis
was caused from a lack of blood flow, there are other stories relating to
arthritis and its simple dissolve meant later in the book at a more
appropriate place, so coming back to observing the body
when you look within it is a spatial feeling and that feeling
is where it's all at, all you have to do is keep your attention on the area as a
witness to it, as an observer, in the beginning when you do this you will be
analytical you cant help yourself, you will be thinking if I understand this
problem where it came from I can help, if I look at it and try to relax my

leg this will help, if I push into it and I push myself into the area I will feel the emotion within it, these are all ideas these are all thoughts that will be there in the early stages of meditation I can only say to you just observe, and feel it back to softness and **comfortableness,** now as you observe yourself

there will be the notion that the person, that's who you think you are is observing the person, so quite rightly you are confused but this is just an illusion , this is part of ignorance, you are pure consciousness pure awareness you are life itself that life is full of peace but it is not full of mental chatter it is just a silent observer, so what you have in the beginning is seemingly a situation where the person is watching the person, and in the end

when you become the master, the master is observing the person, this is called self separation, this is the reason for you observing yourself, again it is called self separation the person will slowly lose identification of itself as the person to realise they are a silent witness, the master, slowly dissolving the chatter the emotion and pain in the body this will be dissolved because the master is observing the noise but in the beginning you think of yourself as a person and in the beginning it seems insane for me to suggest that you are anything else other than that, is this man nuts he must be I can see myself I can feel myself I was born I think I have emotion I am a person, I know it seems ilogical and you can see yourself can feel yourself and you think but the thinking emotional side of yourself is just the front is just the tip of the iceberg is just the personality the ego, so lets come back again to observing yourself, and we are looking at the head as you look at this area you can say in the beginning that pretty much all you have is just confusion chattering noise as you look at your head area you will also feel emotion, emotion that is riddled throughout your body(felt mainly as tightness,tension) you see mind and emotion are as one, they are entwined , if you open the cage door to your Buddgie to give him some freedom in your house but you've left the window open and the budgie escapes that moment for you will also feel guilty they are intertwined so as you think there will be an emotion that goes with it, so hence this front this personality this ego is filled with past events traumas that cause you pain and fill the body with a dead unconscious sluggishness ths is also made worse by knowledge this may sound a very strange thing to say I guess at this point in the book I should warn you that your mind if you're new to mysticism your mind will not like some of what I say because your mind is used to acting like a folder cr in a computer it likes to compartmentalise the things that it hears and reads, and as you move forward, you will have to many times allow yourself to hear thingsopenly that you may not agree with this is simply because your mind wants to keep itself safe and wants to build a shell around itself it likes the status quo the reason knowledge makes us sluggish is because knowledge acts in a certain way firstly when we have knowledge we assume that we know, so once we have this assumption we lose our child like inquisitive nature, one of the things l find most difficult when talking with people is their lack of inquisitiveness and how we tell our children not to .ask so many questions I find it disturbing when I speak to people and there is no childlike inquisitiveness, knowledge is not intelligence, intelligence is what comes out of the moment when you need it right at the point when you need it comes out of the witness out of pure awareness life itself always there its ours it's our master state but when we have assumptions we assume we have knowledge this gets in the way, let me tell you a story a lady came to me in fact she rang me up on the phone it was at the stage when I was a herbalist and iridologist and she said to me I have an ulcer in the top of my palate could I come and see you so that we can sort it out, and I said to her well at this stage I don't know what that is so if you come and I don't know then you can go away and there will be no charge but as I said those words intelligence told me in that moment that the top of the palate relates to the top of the chest cavity and the chest cavity is the area of relationship not getting it off your chest so to speak, and when this lady came it was immediately obvious that I had hit the nail on the head, or intelligence had should I say , this lady was in her 60s and and she had brought a twenty something toyboy and when I told her of my understanding there was an immediate understanding and shaking of heads and some discomfort from the younger chap she went away and rang back the following day and said that the ulcer was virtually gone and there was no pain and she was amazed and very pleased when she came that day there was not only understanding but dissolvement within the chest area because the truth was seen uncovered and made conscious, if anyone thinks that meditation and healing is boring I can assure you that you just need to give it some more time, breakout of any constrictions that you may have place upon yourself,open up to new ideas some of which will seem outlandish positively crazy, when I look back at my life, much of it I have been persecuted for thinking wildly outside of the box and then 10 years later I was being paid to do a talk on the subject, so don't be afraid to always let go of what you assume to be correct and move towards which may seem crazy,

so as your looking into your head in the beginning this noise is so close it seems to be right on top of you you cannot do anything about it ,you cant slow it down but keep persevering move right right into the skull move right into the skull itself get right in and observe every single thought and just keep observing you see what you're actually doing but you don't know it yet, is creating a presence this presence will become stronger and stronger but it's not built overnight this presence will allow you to be present and silent in your own body and the discomfort will drop much quicker, osho used to tell the story of the headmaster and to me it's the most relevant certainly here in this case you are the headmaster but you believe yourself to be all of the children the children wont stop chattering but as you build up more of a presence as the head headmaster you become more of a force to be reckoned with the less the children will chatter, in the beginning when you're in the room they will hardly notice you once you have made your presence felt and you have made it clear in no uncertain terms that you will not be messed about with you are the master ,they will be silent eventually even when you are out of the class they will be silent because the mere thought of your presence is enough to send a shudder down the spine and they will be quiet so this is the same you need to build a presence in your own body I don't know if any of you have been lucky enough to experience the presence of an angel or Sananda or any of the light beings as they move into a room, or if you are at Channelor and they move into your body, but their presence is such that it will always bring tears to your eyes, it makes you shudder as they enter your space the sheer amount of love that they have is so powerful that it brings tears to the eyes, thats what you are creating when you move into your own body space I cannot stress this enough, this is what you're creating you are creating a presence that is powerful enough, as a master and can be present in your own body, and the mind will be still so as you move into your head in the beginning the noise from the children is just crazy non-stop you have to lay down the law you will not stand for it you need to hear every single word from the children every single word they say here it very clearly listen to it allow it to stop, and again hear it again allow it to stop you do not want this noise in your head get in get in there you as master are a force to be reckoned with, a powerful silent loving calm gentle force once you have brought some stillness to the chaos in your head gently bring your attention your presence down to the body and do the same thing, feel the body, in the body you will have especially in the beginning, layer upon layer upon of anxiety, fear,anger, especially in this belly area so as you move down from the head, down into belly the central area bring your attention onto it feel it, in the beginning you are pretty unconscious in the body you can feel very little and I say in the beginning but really even many years down the line you're still uncovering making yourself more conscious you cannot believe how conscious you can become as you move into the body, you see we are saying the body and youll think of it as the body and you will for years go on moving in and moving around what you call the body ,but eventually you will see (feel) the body as a feeling it will just be sensation, so you will be sensational but we will get that at a later stage, for now this is what you're doing is to move around feel your body back to life bringing it back to life just being an observer of the body, being an observer of the head notice how they feel some of you who are our clairvoyant will see colours you will be noticing colours all over the body, but still this is a reflection to some extent of the noise in the body, so don't be too caught up with it colour is a wonderful gift it's great and can be wonderful help in healing yourself and others but remember you're an observer, now with the mind you have thoughts that as you watch them they become still, with the body you will have physical pain and the physical pain will be what you feel first its the grossest, so you may have as we said before physical aches and pains that you may not be able to overcome on your own in the beginning and my suggestion is that you find a local healer if you have pain in the back whatever it may be find a healer who can help dissolve some of the the pain for you, to give you an idea of how much pain you could encounter in the early days for me even after I had been a meditative for a decade I came across Barry long who really put me on this path and the book the main book really that led me to this understanding was stillness is the way and I cannot recommend it highly enough, but for me it took about three years before I had built enough presence to dissolve pain that I had in the back and kidneys and could lie comfortably in bed at night ,this I would suggest is a bit offputting for you so if you have that much pain seek a healer, for me I would lie second after a second and each second was a lifetime I thought I could not stand the pain for another second it would go on and on all night which as I say many of you will find daunting to say the least this is how I learnt about the dis-ease the illness in my own body and then went on to help others in a different way in the early days for me for the first I guess seven tto 10 years I was just a straight hands-on healer I didn't charge, but then it changed for me around this period when I learnt about the body, by looking inside my own, most healers you could say learned to heal someone else before they learn to heal themselves ,they heal themselves usually fromt an external way they take herbs, homeopathy, acupuncture, they go to a therapist in other words they don't go to the root cause of their problem within so don't really understand another body from its root cause they don't understand the source of the problem because they haven't been to the source of the problem in there own body , so if you have pain in your own body go back to it time after time and you will find that it will change, there are two routes in which it will change usually, one it will become more painful and it will have a centre to it , or it will become more diffuse and it will slowly fade away, in the first instance it may become more and more painful and if you look really closely it will have a centre to it's almost like a Pea right in the centre so bring your attention right into   this very central point keep your eye on it don't take your eye off it stay with it and it may seem to you as though this central area is just stable it just wont go but if you see colour you will see the colours change in it and seeing colour in your own body in this way is a fantastic way to treat yourself and others it works quickly on yourself and others and you'll see it move from dark colours through to medium through to light pink etc through to white if for instance you are observing cancer you will see that there is a black centre a and then around this it is red and then outside of this it has a black shell this will change through to the Browns then through to greens blues purple yellow and it will get lighter and lighter until eventually it is white this is how we used to have great success with cancer when my partner who is no longer alive used to observe the cancer itself I would feel the cancer because I am claircentient and she was clairvoyant and the client would also feel or watch the cancer itself but let me stress with cancer it is very difficult for the person themselves to feel it in the beginning or to see it as it is

so unconscious

it has been there for a long time and may well be an entity, it is quite difficult indeed for them to be aware of it but it but works very well when it can be seen and felt by both or three parties and in our case all three would watch it right through to white feel it through to its ending, and this was as much as we could do, if you catch it early enough then you have a good result but if you don't catch it early enough then the result may not be as clear cut, we also ran an animal sanctuary so we had many more animals with cancer than we did with people, at that time I tended to deal with people and my partner dealt with the animal's but let me say for any of you who, and this was always an issue for people when we used to run animal healing courses and human healing courses throughout the country people would always for some reason assume that there is a big difference between being an animal healer and a human healer when you get in under the physical structure of the body you are dealing always with a very similar situation you are dealing with energy colour emotion and thought, when you are talking in terms of thought and emotion for an animal the main problem arises out of the fact that the animals especially if they are a pack or herd animals will be picking up the emotional illness and mental illness of the person the other pack member so the person will be making the animal ill and sometimes people say to me that this sounds a bit hard and a person could feel guilty, I am just saying that this is what we have experienced over the years and if you can understand this and take this on board without it being a personal issue then it is very effective indeed, to give you a some understanding of this at this point let me tell you of a dog with epilepsy the owner rang us up and at this point in my life we used to run a phone in diagnosis for animals, and the woman rang about her dog that was having epileptic fits three or four times a day and the vet and was prescribing stronger and stronger drugs and the problem was getting worse and he was not expected to live much longer , and she had nowhere to go and so we told her what we do and explained on the phone that the dog would be having fits because it was picking up emotion from someone in

the family and that if we could treat the family member and they
understood where the problem was arising and we also treated the dog
then there would be no more fits so the girl with her parents drove down
from the Midlands down to the West Country with the dog and I
remember when it arrived had to be hosed off as it had had a fit in the
back of the car and poo,d itself we duly treated the dog and the girl when I
say treated I mean that we dissolved the emotion in the dog and dissolved
the emotion in the girl until there was so much peace and softness and
stillness in the girl and the dog that we knew we had a good result, the dog
was out for the count and I remembered we actually carried out to the car,
a few days later they said all was well and we suggested to them that they
would need to come off of the drugs slowly take a sharp knife and slowly
cut away a piece of the pill until the dog was taking no pills about two years
later we got alovely letter from them saying that the dog had died in an
accident but had never had a fit from that day to the day he died, the girl
herself became much more aware of her stress levels and would ensure
that she would keep her distance from the dog should she get stressed,and
she would definitely not sleep anywhere near the dog and would preferably
let the dog sleep at the far end of the house from her bedroom so let's
come back to the meditation let's talk about another issue and that is
whether we need candles and incense, figures etc, and even a special area
of the house or garden all a very personal thing some people who may
have had past lives when this was important feel a need for this and it can
certainly be helpful in terms of creating a peaceful atmosphere that will
kickstart your meditation so if you feel this it is something that you need
then that's good, if not no problem, eventually you would be looking at
the meditative state twenty four seven even if you are up to your arse in
alligators it is certainly helpful to have an area that is peaceful and is used
time and time again because the energy of your meditation will embed
itself in the chair, in the area itself, again this is something that may be new
to you but chairs and beds are areas of emotion that you may not be aware

of, let me explain when we were on   holiday to Portugal a few years ago
we rented a villa and when sleeping in bed had terrible backache until we
slept in a different mattress and then it was fine, now that was one instance
among thousands and to a normal Western mind you would say the
mattress was simply uncomfortable too hard or too soft but this is not the
case , a few years ago I spent a while sleeping in the back of my pickup on
rolled up newspapers and even though the bottom of the pickup had
ridges in it and it was midwinter I still got a good nights sleep with no back
problems and after all the years that I have put into understanding my
body I can assure you that you will find the same in years to come once
you open up to energy and emotion, so if you have a peaceful area that you
choose as your meditation area, your meditation room, that would be
really good but not essential, now place your feet firmly into the ground by
this I mean imagine your feet falling down into the ground, you see as a
native person your body would be used to energy coming up through your
feet up into your body rising right up through your body out through the
top of your head and washing you free of emotion keeping it clean, but in
our Western society, modern world, we have become unnatural and rarely
connect with nature we become disconnected from the energy of the earth
so drop your feet down into the ground and become aware of the soles of
your feet and what you'll find is that in the beginning your feet may well be
and it's most likely that they will be, separate from the Earth itself from the
ground itself in other words you can feel this separation between you and
the ground but this will disappear as energy comes up through rises up
from the earth up into your body, see if you can feel this change as it
happens so keep your attention be attentive to your feet lower legs, it is
very subtle and see if you can feel this tingly change in your feet and legs as
the energy starts to move up your legs and into your body and you will
become aware of a lack of separation between you and the earth   your feet
will merge with the Earth and you will become one with it
as the energy moves up through,

in the same way as if you have a plug and socket and you push the plug into the socket and flick the switch energy will move from the socket into the plug and they will become energetically one and the same this is the same for you and the earth you're plugging yourself into the energy of the Earth, allowing it to move up through the body allowing it to rise slowly up the body dissolving the emotion as it rises up when it reaches the base centre that is your lower back in other words ,if you are attentive just keep your eye on it feel it you will notice possibly a slight slow beat over the years this beat will become more conscious and you will be able to feel it really well likewise as it rises up to the next centre you will feel that, and then the next, you will feel that right up to the top of your head right up to the Crown centre itself you will be able to feel this energy rising up from the ground slowly dissolve the emotion as it rises bringing your energy centres back to life so that you have this lovely soft flow of energy from the ground, from the Earth rising all the way up and moving out through the top of the head the beat in the base centre is quite slow I would say two seconds apart (but this changes when opening) its quite difficult when I try to put it into seconds but the base centre would be about two seconds , but can be quicker between the beats and then each centre as you come up through the body gets a little quicker a little bit faster until the Crown centre is really fast indeed, you will all probably have seen the pictures of the energy centres within the body and from my point of view I do not wish to go into too much detail of exactly where they are and their names and colours because this is something that you may get caught up in with your head, dealing with the exact area, am I doing something wrong , is which centre is this, why is this one closed, etc all of that heady stuff is too much you just want to feel the gentle pulse the gentle beat by being attentive firstly from the base centre and when you feel a little beat a little pulse then move a little bit higher, up to the general area of the bellybutton, see if you can feel another one there and then you will have two pulses that you can feel although of course in the beginning it just will not be clear but there will definitely be something there and eventually you can feel it, and then you will be able to feel three and four going right up through but be patient with yourself don't worry about this idea that you will have, am I doing it right , I must be doing something wrong, this is a very common normal idea that people have this idea that they are somehow doing something wrong, they are not doing something right, they must be silly, they must be slow, they must have read the wrong books, why is it not happening to me, all of that is mental chatter all of that is the mind trying to keep you occupied and whilst it is doing so you will not feel because you are thinking so be gentle with yourself and just gently, gently, be attentive very softly , gently I cannot stress this enough the feelings in the body the changes in the body are very subtle, very subtle indeed, for the Western mind to grasp so the more gentle you are with yourself the more patient you are just keep observing be alert if your mind is a problem for you push right in to it get right inside, feel your head, become really, really,aware of the thoughts themselves become very very conscious of all of the thoughts again be patient with yourself you're not doing something wrong and in the beginning you must remember that you identify yourself as the person of the head ,the centre of yourself is in the head. it should be, and will be eventually in the belly area, in the beginning the centre of yourself is in the head you are off balance your centre is not in the centre it out at the periphery at the shallow periphery of yourself so you will be used to constantly over and over thinking analysing and doing and you will not be comfortable with this idea of non-doing just observing ,without doing, and this is the meditation process itself just to be an observer of all tightness all of the thoughts all of the emotion in the body, which you won,t feel as emotion necessarily, you may feel anxiety in the beginning for instance you may feel this subtle fear that is in your belly but 98% of the emotion that is rattling around your body or should I say not really rattling around your body but stagnant, fixed within your body, is very stable nearly all of this emotion you will be unaware of but you will be aware of it when you look within you will be aware of it as tightness as tension, your shoulders will be tight your neck will be tight your shoulders for instance will be up around your ears and your ears will be down around your shoulders, just observe it see how your neck is pulling your head down and your shoulders are up, everybody is different everybody will have a different way in which they hold themselves and each person will see something different within their body, and after a while this will become utterly fascinating when I sit with someone and I observe their body and I tell them about their body and ask them, do you see that ,do you see how your your knees are up around your ears your pulling your legs up with the stress, or you're holding your head down real tight your right arm are is pulled up and across your left shoulder all sorts of strange ways in which we hold ourselves but we are unconscious of, and then a person will see this and then this ,becoming conscious of process, will begin the process of dissolvement if they become truly conscious of it let's say for instance I sit with them and that's my job to bring it to consciousness then this problem will dissolve very quickly you could say it will dissolve before the end of the session or within seconds, if you sit with this problem yourself you see that your knees are pulling up as it is quite a common thing where the tension is in the tops of the legs or the backs of the legs and you are holding your legs up for instance then you would may have to sit with it time and time and time again until you become strong enough present enough focused enough to dissolve this, and that is what meditation is about, becoming conscious of the unconscious becoming conscious of this pain this emotion this noise that you are carrying that has been placed there unconsciously in the past with the passage of time they get locked in and they could be there for a year, 10 years 40 years or 4000 years from past lives let me give you a small example to illustrate this, some friends came to see us and I believe it was about their cat in fact it was one of the cats who had a bone marrow problem, and they came into the kitchen and the chappy was a therapist and as he came into the kitchen I had to more or less grab my heart as the pain was intense, and I had to leave the room go out in the garden and get a grip, and and then I went back into the kitchen, the chap was telling the story of how a few days earlier he had watched his other cat die as it went under a car and his grief and guilt was unbearable and this had locked into his heart and given him a severe, to him unconscious heart problem, I could give you a thousand stories that are similar that affect all parts of the body from the top of your head to the bottom of your feet and beyond out into your aura, they will give you a damaged aura all or most of these things you will be unconscious of,until you then have a physical problem, at a later stage you will go to see a doctor or a therapist who will diagnose you in the way that they understand, the way they have been taught if it is a doctor it will be in the shallowest way possible so they will only talk in terms of the physical body the blood the organs etc if it is a therapist then it will be in different ways and they may approach upon a mental emotional issue but they will still give you herbs or change of diet or homoeopathy etc all of these things are good but do you see they don't really address the initial, and I stress it's the initial causal factor and there is a great need into today's world for people to simply be conscious of the initial causing factor within an illness to go right back to the cause itself, dissolve the cause in a quiet soft energetic way so that the person is free of the physical symptoms free of the pain job done, let's come back to the energy its rising up through the body gently do you see how your feet are changing do you see how your feet are now merging with the Earth, if they are not merging with the Earth if for instance you feel the the heel of your foot is hard then this will be because you have very low energy you may need a serious rest , bring your attention right down into, take yourself not with your head with your feeling right down into the heels of your feet feel them back to life, how do they feel, what do they feel like, feel feel , feel the ground, feel just above the hardness feel that keep your attention on it feel it, feel it, feel it, stay with it and it will change what does the sole feel like what does the ball feel like   is that soft, is that softer than the heel I need to be careful here because you will be used to being analytical and I know it sounds analytical but I am talking awareness, the attention of, feel it, so don't think in terms   of my foot is this or that   etc, keep the mind out of it feel your body feel the   energy when I ask people to do this in a group they very often ask   me if I mean imagine and they get confused they think that I am talking about imagining your feet but I am not, I am saying feel your feet, not imagine we are so unused to being feeling, and having an unconscious body that even the idea of bringing your body back to life by feeling it is difficult to grasp, so in other words if I put a nail into the centre of your hand and just press it into the centre of your palm you can feel that nail you can feel the pain, imagination is is a totally different ball game so you are feeling your feet feeling the energy rise up through your legs up into your body bringing it back to life, let's look at something else that often arises and that is the mind suggesting to you that you are doing something wrong or that you are not doing something right, or that you must be slow you haven't read enough books so you're obviously not doing it in the correct way and this is all just a way for the mind to keep you busy and occupied you are so fully identified with being the mind the person that is it is inconceivable at this stage for you to grasp that you are the sensation the feeling the energy and not the thought , coming back to the headmaster you're so fully identified with being the children in the class always noisy always running riot in your head and are mostly unconscious of this, that you do not realise that you are the headmaster and it's your presennce as the master that will bring this body to stillness release it of its tightness and its hardness and its discomfort and its pain this presence is hard earned in the beginning you enter the classroom and the children are still noisy and running riot but you just stand and watch and wait maybe bring a book down onto a table and slowly but surely the children will become quiet, and eventually even the thought of you entering the room will be enough they will be quieter and quieter and less unruly and you will identify yourself as the master and even though you may have bad days where you will forget that you are the master and you will enter the class and the class will still be loud   and rowdey still you are the master, you get a wage at the end of the week to prove it you are a fully paid-up member of the headmaster's union, you will have your off days a lot but eventually those off days will become fewer as your identification slowly changes   this will come at the latter stages of meditation as you move from the head to the belly so for now patients, and perseverance the ability to be present as a presence is hard-won and in the beginning is a very hard learning curve, even the very idea of meditation is difficult if not impossible to understand because you are hearing about meditation from your ears to your mind not from your ears to your belly and your mind doesn't understand what is beyond, it can,t   understand no mind you have no point of reference, so this is why the only way to understand meditation to understand stillness,is the experience of it even to understand a body without aches and pains and without hardness and stress is easier with hindsight , you will slowly become more still your body will slowly become freer of emotion and pain and hardness a bit like the hands of the clock it will be slowly slowly every day a new point of reference will be different and difficult to remember remember the golden rule try to keep your reading material to that of Masters as your central theme , read other books but make sure that you read and keep coming back to a master or Masters and their cd s or MP3 thingies, we have covered quite a bit on these early stages although you must be aware that I have given you no technique no hard and fast rules so this will seem to you as though I have given you nothing, this will be the hardest to understand is this, taking away process, rather than an adding on to process, if you go to a workshop and they give you lots to remember lots of knowledge that you need to store and you get a bit of paper at the end of it there is much for you to remember let's say for instance you go and do a Reiki course you will need to remember symbols there will be hand placements that you must remember all of this will be given great importance you will be given much that you must read in books, and this must be struck to rigidly and your mind will love this and enjoy it because you feel like you have gained something, meditation true meditation is the opposite if this,no new knowledge new learning, it is a dissolving of the ego of your assumptions of your current subjectivity of who you think you are it is a dissolving of your knowledge much of what you wish to hang onto and think you know will need to be dissolved, you will need to be confused because confusion is a breakdown you will need to be less , less noise, less emotion in the body, less stiffness less tightness less ache and pain all of this is the opposite of what you have been used to up to this point in your life and this is vital that you have an understanding of this as this is the opposite to what you are used to, it is intelligence rather than knowledge, knowledge is gained in parrot fashion by reading books or from others externally from the world it is second-hand it may be hundreds of years old and it may or may not be true, intelligence is always correct it is instantaneous in the moment it comes through emptiness when you need it, it is there   the purpose of meditation is to bring about a situation where the the body is as clear as glasss so that intelligence has no impedance by this sludge that we build up over the years, meditation is this gradual process of washing away all the pain and noise of the past, losing and in losing, gaining peace, stillness, intelligence, wisdom, kindness, softness, understanding and empathy the list is endless, you will not like this but all emotion is negative, if you read middle of the road new-age material you will have an idea, concept that learning from emotion is good and that emotion itself is actually good you will say but what about love, love is not an emotion it is your underlying state of being, what about happiness, happiness is transitory it comes and goes with unhappiness however those childlike moments when you felt elation that is your underlying state, so it is dissolving what is not real on the surface so that you are left with the underlying state, that is what meditation is all about, and when you think of the work involved in meditation and how hard it is, how difficult it is to understand, anything to do with it, the rewards need to be great , we could just to go for a formal religion were all we have to do is sit down or get down onto our knees say a few prayers and feel really pleased because , job done, and all we have to do is act nicely especially on Sundays surely that would be a much easier path than meditation well of course that's only acting it's not real, Jesus does not want us to act as he did he wishes us to understand that we are as he is , he wishes us to uncover that truth and walk that difficult path towards self mastery as well, it is not easy it requires immense amounts of perseverance and an underlying passion that is coming through from your essential being something deep inside will push and push and push and what will happen in the early stages the middle stages and the later stages is that you will be given a gift you will be given a glimpse of what is to come so that you can then move towards that as a more permanent state a story comes to mind a gift I was given, I used to go to Iona for three weeks in May and meet up with many like-minded people and we would all have a big gathering, in the three-week period may be 200- 300 people and I was sat with someone on a beach the beach with the special stones and if you'v been to Iona you probably know the beach I mean and it so happened that on this day I merged with osho and I was a gibbering wreck because his presence was so so unbelievably soft that all I could manage were the words it's so soft, it is so soft, my body was virtually horizontal I could hardly hold myself up and it was as much as I could do to speak very very softly as osho himself does to this person, over the years there been glimpses ,a gift of the future, although I consider myself quite harsh, even now with hindsight I look back to my early days I am like a kitten in comparison do not imagine that because you read spiritual books you do courses, you become a Reiki Master or you meditate that you will all of a sudden overnight lose all of your pain in the ass human traits, you have become an egos it is normal the path back to ego lessness is not an overnight process don't try to hide your traits your habits that you are not proud of the more you hide them the deeper they will go the darker they become the more divided a personality you will be you will become more cunning, and brittle, and viscous, instead become as conscious as you can of these traits just an observer of them un judging un suppressing in this way you will avoid becoming more complex in your ego you can only act nicely for a while and then you will explode with all that you have hidden, and you will also become very sensitive to self-criticism as you were hiding so much and also do not imagine that those who you meet who are taking a course running a group are healers or psychics or write books are somehow better than you, it is not the case until we are free of ego we all suffer with and struggle with our human traits it is an evolutionary stage that we must go through learn from become conscious of and then it falls away that's all we can ask is that things will fall away when they are mature enough when they have been seen fully and made conscious this is the process that happens when we face something within the body to make this process of dissolvement Easier we need to look at a few tools to help the process one of which is the breath if we experiment with the breath whilst observing feeling the body you will notice that you will change the inner landscape quite quickly and dramatically by just altering your breath one of the best ways to do this is the broken breath technique whereby the you break your breath in a completely random and unorderly way very gently at first just keep that up whilst your attention is within the body keep that broken breath going for a matter of 1-2 minutes and then stop and you will see that you may feel a little sick little queasy your body will be buzzing and all you've done is just randomly broken your breath in a way that is similar to the breath that you would have if you were sobbing,it is a kind of sobbing breath in and out in no pattern at all, what this does is break up the emotional content within the body so that it can then be dissolved and the best way to release this broken emotion is to then throw your breath out bring your breath back in

again and then throw your breath out again do this three or four times
take a break then throw your breath out again for another three or four
times and that will release the emotion that has been stirred up in the body
this is a tremendously simple powerful way to just gently release the body
of the buildup of emotion, emotion that builds up over the years and is
also emotion that builds up daily whether it be during the day when you're
at work or at night even when you're dreaming, emotion will be building
up all of the time I know this may sound a bit of an exageration but that's
just the way it is as a human being, so as you gain the ability to release
emotion from your body remembering that as you release from the body
you are also really releasing it from the head as well because it will come
up and hit you in the mind so if you have for instance guilt within the body
that guilt will come up and give you guilty thoughts so you're not only
releasing from the body you,r releasing it from torturing you in your mind
as well, so whenever you are able able do this gentle breath technique
again remember no structure to the breath at all don't do it for too long
because if you do you, you will make yourself sick , it only makes you feel
sick in the beginning because of the amount of emotion that is in the body
after a few months of doing this you will find that you can throw your
breath about as much as you like and you will be relatively unaffected by
any feeling of sickness, but you also feel at this time a strong desire not to
do this, it is a very strange and powerful feeling that you just don't want to
do any breath work, if you find that you have emotion that you can actually
recognise, remember that a lot of the time we just don't know that we are
feeling emotional but if you have emotion that you simply say is anger or
frustration or what have you just simply go straight and throw that out
with the breath throw out bring your breath in throw it out, it's throwing
out of the breath that is important because you're throwing out the
emotion, if you play with breath when you're meditating just play with this
simple technique you will find that let's say for instance you have a pain in
your body and you move right into that pain you watch it and then you

start to break up your breath and throw out and you continue watching the pain you will find that the pain will change, for instance if it is a fairly hard painful area that you just can't crack if you break your breath and throw out, break your breath and throughout, just gently you'll find that the pain itself will change if its what I call diffuse it will either get harder and harder and tighter and tighter and more painful and will have a centre to it that you can almost grasp like a pea, or it will will become more and more diffuse it will just go softer and softer and softer , and then you will find if you go away and relax and chill out then when you come back and look at it again that the pain will be less it will have settled to a lesser degree, when you have developed quite a presence you will be dissolving the pain of the past and this will constantly bring up pain in the body and this pain is sandwiched in with layers of anger and anger can be quite a problem especially for your partner because you'll just find you are Snappy, angry, you don't know why, you don't know where it came from it will creep up on you, you will just be snappy and I'm sorry but this is just part of the process you are uncovering layers decades hundreds of years of pain that has gone in and settled into your body, you'll also find that you may if you have dissolved a lot get cystitis or diarrhoea you will burp a lot and you will find that your body will change in ways that in the beginning you will not understand you will have an ache or pain that you didn't have may not have had the day before and you could say all this is doing me no good, that's not the case it is simply stirring up all of the underlying sludge if the sludge is left there it will affect you the rest of your life you need to get rid of it, but at the same time you need to learn how to get rid of it how to cope with it how to understand it, let me tell you a story about how things really started to change for me it was maybe the early 90s and a friend of ours came down the track and said to me that she had just been to see and I'm pretty sure it was Barbara Marciniac and she had done a one-week course with Barbara and the Angels and this was very unusual for this lady but she said to me, it was all about what you talk about but I just don't understand it or didn't understand it can you tell me how I can create my centre and I remember at the time that I was under the bonnet of car and my hands were covered in oil so I went indoors and cleaned up and my character is such that I like to get straight down to the job and get it done and not mess about , it's just a part of my character, I'm pretty straightforward and to the point so I said okay right let's sit down, she sat opposite me and I said okay now let's take a shufti at your centre see what's there and as I said that I exploded I became 100 foot tall I was golden I was filled with bliss and to cut a long story short I said to her as we finished well I don't know what it was like for you but the earth moved for me and she laughed and said yes the same for me she also had exploded, shortly after this we had one of our usual weekly meetings and I found that when I spoke to someone and I spoke to the group I was utterly and completely overwhelmed by the emotion and at the time I just didn't understand what I was feeling and why I was feeling so much and didn't know how to deal with it but basically what was happening was that I was feeling their emotion which was also bouncing off of mine, so it then took many years learning how to decipher and cope and help others with the emotion that is within the body and how this creates a tightness within the body, especially for everyone in the head and neck and shoulder areas, and let me say at this point and put it on a page of its own

Until you dissolve the tightness the hardness and the stiffness
that is in the head and neck and shoulder area you will never really understand energy, and egolesness

In the early stages of meditation your neck head and shoulders will be tight filled with emotion and very very difficult for you to dissolve even with help from a healer who can place their hands on your neck and shoulders to help you dissolve this area, you will still keep on making yourself tight on a daily basis when you eventually keep it soft you will really be able to understand egolessness this energy will rush into the brain area the energy centres in the head will come to life and it will be much easier for you to understand and move forward with meditation so at this point let's reiterate what we said earlier in the book find a healer and allow them to give you healing as often as you can because this will dissolve much of your past, you see the deeper the pain that you have it may be further back in your past it may have been there 10,000 years, could be a bit too much for you to take every time you go you just can't get past the pain you may give up and not meditate again so get some help from a healer ,and the daily stuff that you build up is much quicker and easier to dissolve, say half an hour to an hour I know that sounds a long time and in the beginning what you can do for yourself to dissolve your own stuff does take a while it's not quick but slowly you'll learn you will understand you,ll create a presence you'll be more able to be still and present in the moment free of thought and gain power and light in your own energy centres enough to become quicker and quicker at the job, do you think that a master becomes a master overnight easily how do you think they gained understanding, there is this notion this misunderstanding that enlightenment happens in a moment easily and by chance, and so there is no movement towards that enlightenment if you see what I mean, but the truth is of course enlightenment does happen in a moment, but prior to that moment the person had to go through much experiment and anxt and pain and understanding and inner work in the same way that a martial arts master has had years and years of practice and understanding and inner work, there are great similarities between martial arts and meditation maybe not so much in some Western dojos as there is in the East, just before we finish this first section of the book let's look at a few other tools that are available to help the first one that comes to mind are the crystals malachite and azurite which often come together in the same stone malachite is good for absorbing emotion azurite is good at absorbing mental noise together if you sit with them in your hand you will notice a real calming affect as they absorb, interesting isn't it that copper is smelted from malachite and copper is used for arthritis ,and arthritis is from my experience emotion based , another one that also has this effect is aquamarine, rose quartz is great for many negative emotional states let me tell you again a short story about rose quartz, I am not a great

lover of the British winter and I remember many years ago I used to suffer
with a lower back problem due to resentment of the weather i came in one
lunchbreak and could hardly stand up because my lower back was playing
up and grabbed a piece of rose quartz and shoved it near my lower back
and by the time i had finished my lunchbreak my back was as soft as a
puddun and I was less of a resentfull arsehole if you have the right crystal
for the right job they are fantastic smoky quartz is another great help I
suggest if you are not too knowledgeable on crystals to buy yourself a book
and do a little study they can be very helpful the Bach flower remedies
likewise can be a great help to help you cope with the emotions that you
will face, osho,s Mystic Rose technique is a wonderful technique for
reducing drastically the amount of debris that you carry, it can be found in
his book ,meditation the first and last freedom, it is a bit drastic for most
people as it requires three hours of laughing for seven days then three
hours of crying for seven days or vice versa and three hours of meditation
for seven days most people could not manage this but you could cut it
down in time, the peace that you will feel after even your first session is
un-believable to cry solidly for three hours releases decades of pain and
another of osho,s techniques that is really helpful are no mind technique
which is basically talking gibberish or nothing that can be understood for
an hour a day this may sound crazy but it releases a buildup of mental
noise and again has a wonderful effect the other technique which I like
from the book is kundalini which even when it is very gently worked
allows the body to release energetic buildup which has been there for years.
Barry long is very much straight to the point and has some great material
his book stillness is the way will assist a huge amount towards your stop
thinking campaign it is a three cd compilation , whereas with osho when
you listen to his voice it is like honey dripping from the wings of a
butterfly on a sunny day, with Barry long when you listen to his voice it is
more like your old headmaster telling you to be quiet they have a different
flavour but they both do a great job we have just about come to the end

of this first section on the beginning stages of meditation of course there is no point at which you are a beginner and then you move on to the middle stages there is no line in the sand and in terms of length of time when pressed on the subject Barry long used to often use the idea of becoming fluent in a language I quite like that explanation as it is very difficult to put a time on meditation matters and also if you say that it will take years and years even decades you would be putting an idea into somebody's head when it is better not to so now lets move into the middle stage

THE MIDDLE STAGE OF MEDITATION

How would you define the end of the first stage the beginning of the middle I'm not sure that you could or that you would want to I have separated the book up into this in this way simply so that I can talk more in depth about the nner world in a subtler way in a way that you cant t really understand in the early days it like maturing cheese it just doesn't happen over night what you can understand after three for five years meditation or 10years of meditation is different than you can understand upfront, your subjectivity will change you will work in a different way in your body hopefully you're still there still meditating every day, hopefully your meditationw ill be over a longer period a little more profound, let's deal with maybe oneof the most difficult issues you can face in this middle period which is the understanding intellectually that you should be in the belly, you read it enough times but for you it is still not happened or should we say happening and you feel that you're doing something wrong because the belly still isn't active you don't really understand why, this can be a real difficult one to get your head around because you read it in all the books that you should be in the belly, but when you look at yourself you can see that you are still based in the head and yet somehow it just doesn't happen so let's really take this apart and see if we can explain and explore this issue firstly I guess we need to look at head neck and shoulders are your head neck and shoulders soft or are they still rigid, the reason i. ask this is because as I said previously if this area is not soft then you simply won,t understand the way in which energy works in the body softness

needs to enter the head and shoulders and neck so that you become energetic there and then you will drop, are you soft, free of tension when you ar e the belly will begin to work in a way that it's never really worked in before, it will have a real beat to it that you will be able to feel and you will be able to move sensationally , rather than mentally trying to , and of course it is a big

difference when you're trying to bring your belly to life what happens of course is that you're trying from the head so your shooting yourself in the foot the more you try the more you will be based there, so if you are housed in the head how tight is your head neck and shoulders let's take this as our first looking in sit as you normally do backup right feet on the ground you will be less worried about you posture now you know that you can even if you wanted to, do this lying in bed, or in the sun lounger, you know you will not fall asleep, do this sitting on the loo, driving the car, and hopefully you've spread out from just meditating on the chosen time each day, so your feet are on the ground you can feel nicely merged with the earth just check out the shoulders the neck and the head, how do they feel now let's move into feeling not thinking about, really get to grips with this understanding this very subtle understanding that we are talking about feeling not imagination, not thinking about your shoulders, but feeling your shoulders, your neck, you can do a comparison and this is really quite useful and helpful campare the feeling in the neck area with the feeling in the let's say for instance your legs , do your legs feel tension the same as your shoulders, it's likely that what you will feel is that your legs are a little tingly softish no great amount of tightness any more because you've looked at them softened them down, although at this stage we need to just talk about the legs, over many lifetimes when you're faced with a situation of fight or flight as we have been in those days of many centuries ago when life was much more physical and dangerous we were often faced with situations where we had to stand and fight when we really wanted to run and so the legs themselves can be filled with lots of tension and tightness left over from fight or flight so when you say l compare them with the legs your legs may or may not be softer than your neck and again this is great because it still gives you this comparison they may be as tight as your neck if you closely look at them or they may be well melted from the Earth energy that has been coming up into the calfs made its way up just about to the knees but not gone any further and I would ask you at this stage is this the case so your feet maybe nicely soft and all and spongy ,do they have emotion within is there a feeling under the sensation, if you have the sensation on the surface of tightness or pain or discomfort then under that within that, can you feel the emotional content within that area is it clean stay , watch, really go to town on just feeling that area, what we're doing is we're trying to for instance do a comparison between the lower legs and this shoulder area, so let's look into those lower legs really check them out, as we do this in this middle stage of meditation where we go that one step further we are not just looking at the physical sensation that maybe there the tightness or hardness or pain or discomfort on the surface but what's going on underneath, and in doing this we need to use words which are more subjective and it will get progressively more difficult to talk about what's going on inside because the words we use will be words we,v maybe never used before because were moving into a new area if we say for instance that an orange tastes like a lemon but less bitter we're doing the best we can to describe this taste sensation, so as we move into the body what were also doing is to use words as best we can, to use almost a flavour what is the flavour the feeling under the tightness, and so to the shoulders do they have emotion under the tightness, can you feel the emotion, and if so do you feel it in the shoulders or in your belly, in other words you may feel the emotion of the shoulders but the emotional sensation of it will be felt in the belly , and as you feel it can you go beyond feeling it as such and such part of your body, just sensation , not a body part , so okay were looking into the shoulder area and the chances are you will feel that there is still some tightness it's not 100% slack and easy and comfortable you may not feel the emotion because that emotion is very difficult to grasp in your own body, funnily enough if I am dealing with somebody else's body in exactly the same way it is much easier to feel there emotion, because it's not emotion I,v become unconscious of, now with the shoulders it's highly likely that your shoulders are pulling up and your head is scrunched down and that's how you hold yourself all the time but you've never really been aware of it, that's how you release it by becoming conscious of it now another thing that will happen is that as you watch you will find that it will grow tighter and tighter and tighter and tighter and then just just release and slacken and then again it will go tighter and tighter and tighter and then just release and that's what will happen, don't go forcing anything just watch it fascinated by it, this tightening process and its slackening, and every time it slacks off it will never be quite that tight again because you were becoming conscious, more conscious than ever before and you're bringing it to life, and it will hold just that little bit less tension than it did before, because of its shape you have the wide shoulders coming into the narrow neck, emotion in the body tends to rise up from the belly or lower back you'll feel fear down in the belly anxiety and it   rises up through the chest and and then gets restricted in the neck, that's why the neck shoulder area is such a difficult and the last area to be really tackled and overcome because you're always having a situation where anxiety etc rises up like smoke and gets congested in the neck, and eventually makes its way up into the head , as it makes its way past the throat you will find yourself snappy with words and as it finds its way up into the head itself you'll have negative thoughts because you've got negative emotion making its way up to the head ,we ought to mention the moon you need to watch the moon because the moon has an effect on the body a large effect on the body you may be a little sceptical but watch the way you feel on a full moon for instance on the run up to the full moon and I'm not talking precision here so many people say oh it can't be the moon because it's not the full moon the full moon is at 12:10 on Thursday that is thinking in a fundamental mental way it's not like that, approximately 7 days before the full moon you will start to feel the moon itself you will be affected by and feel your problem areas so if your main problem is a worry over cash then you will begin to feel worried more and more as the moon progresses and you will also feel it in your body in the area that corresponds to your worries so if for instance you have a worry of cash you will feel it in your knees because this is the area where you support yourself you'll feel it in your ankles , you will be just walking down the street and they will give you jab , as you worry your knees your hips and even your lower back , or your belly will feel anxiety and this will make you snappy and moody simply because the moon is moving towards full and that's the way it's affecting you, the new moon is the same but it has the effect of seven days after the moon so when you see that little sliver of the moon that's when you're affected and usually a little under the seven days I find with the new moonn it's more like five days after the new you will feel this emotional discomfort, storms are the same, the weather itself will affect you greatly but you haven't noticed it before, let's talk about them bring them out in the open, you should be open enough now to at least hear it and not pooh-pooh it, hear it, be open to it, observe it, and watch it in your own body, the natives knew all of these things and watched them and worked with them in a way that Western culture would find difficult to embrace so this is not new, we need to understand our body in a larger holllistic way we are part of the planet merge with it feel it puts your shoulds and shoul,nts to one side let me give you an idea of what I mean this chappy that i. told you about before who gave me the tapes and had lived with osho also was a chauffeur for Barry long and he was at Barry longs talk one day and Barry long was thrown about the stage because a storm was coming and it would be all too easy to say oh that happen toshouldn't a master but do not assume that you know what the next stage is like or how you should behave, that is an ego centric idea subjective shoulds and should,nts some of the things that have happened to me in the past I could have easily closed down to them if I had said that can't possibly be so, and this is what most people do, so just be fully open, so for instance with storms you will find that if one is two or three hours away you may be extremely angry and upset, because that storm is coming don't blame yourself just observe your reaction and notice how when the storm comes your stormy and afterwards you feel the calmness that follows, so we were looking at this neck shoulder area and have tension as the emotion that rises up through the body, maybe starting in the belly, it is quite amazing if you are fully conscious of your body how much anxiety is there, for so much of the time, you're anxious when you get out of bed and it may be just something simple that is playing on your mind you have to open up shop your the first one in you know you have to get there before nine o'clock you have to be there before anyone else stands outside the door, if you don't open on time somebody will moan and then when you have opened up it is usually not so bad because you are actually in action and not just thinking about the future and usually when you are taking action that is the very best you can do because you no longer need to think of the future but throughout the day you will notice that time and time again you may be anxious you may be anxious when you're dealing with different people in your office, around your building site there maybe somebody there that you don't like and every time you had to deal with them it affects you emotionally, so throughout one single day you can have an awful lot of emotion people often think that the only emotion that they have within their week is when they have an argument or when they have road rage or something similar but it's not the case throughout the day you will be effected by emotion in your body and throughout the night when you have a dream that dream will often be unpleasant and you will be again effected by emotion and when you watch the tv if you're watching even a mild thriller let alone a horror movie you will be storing emotion, the tv is a fantastic way to release the emotion in your shoulders because if you are watching just a very mild programme you will notice that as the person in the movie gets in trouble or you feel that something is about to happen your shoulders will be up around your ears and you had been unconscious of it is a good way to get grips with your body watch the tv and be conscious of your stress it is a good way to meditate you are sat still and you are being drawn into this program, watch but stay in your body that way you will learn how to be conscious other than when you are sitting to meditate at your allotted time you will draw it out into other areas of your life and tv is great because you will be sitting for 2-3 hours in the evening or more in the winter and you can be observing yourself whilst observing the tv you can be feeling your body feel what it's like as you watch different programs and as you watch a thriller watch how your body tenses up it's a great way to expand your awareness and become more conscious there is a story that gurdieff crashed his car so that he could be fully conscious and aware within the crash itself before during and after and it was a serious crash this may sound Way too much you, you would think this is bonkers but this is the kind of awareness that you will need to expand into as your meditation becomes more of an awareness than the meditation that you do in a short time slot, so in the beginning you sit for 10 min half an hour one hour and do your meditation, do being the operative word, then you realise that the doing is a problem the doer is the problem then you start to break out into this situation where you become more conscious and aware in other areas of your life you can become aware when you are on the loo because you are sat and you are still, you can become conscious when you are driving because again you may be sat and still for a long period, but even so you will need to be patient with yourself because you need to remember, when your walking just walk , in other words you need to make an effort to remind yourself to be conscious when you are usually unconscious, you need to remember to be aware of the fact that you are driving so let's check out my body so it's still something that you have to make an effort to do and remember its not yet a natural process, and it is just not easy to remember it more often than not you will forget, but keep persevering and eventually you reach a stag

where you realise that you are the awareness itself you have reached a tipping point where you just simply realise that you are the stillness you are the awareness you are the master and then it becomes easier to be aware more often and with less effort and all of your sweat and tears have come to fruition

When you reach this stage then you could say that this is the point at which you are reaching the later stages of Meditation, you simply really do realise that you are master even though you cock up all the time you forget yourself you become unconscious you go back to thinking, somehow beings still and being aware has now become equal to or more than the thinking

But from now we are looking at this effort that you need to make on a daily basis time after time to remember to be aware, you will forget more than you remember, so be patient with yourself it is very much like a diet you will fail more than you succeed and it is very easy to give up and say it's impossible how can I possibly change my whole persona to be aware more through out the day, the difference between a master and a non master is a master has simply gained the ability of being conscious and realised that he is this conscious awareness free of thought all of the time and like gurdgieff and like you and me they had to go through this stage of remembering reminding themselves kicking themselves, the book that I bought in Brisbane all those years ago refered to ,when walking just walk when talking just talk above all don't wobble, in the early stages mind must remember to watch mind that's what it seems like, come the end, stillness is being disturbed by thought is what you know, subtle but huge difference, experimentation looking in to all of the things that you are doing they did as well and more besides, so coming back to the shoulders they will be stiff tight unmoving under this deadness will be emotional stagnation a pond of stagnant emotion very difficult for you to feel this emotion so break your breath breath out as you look in to this area, look in look in, stay there, feel it, break your breath experiment see how it feels see how it changes see how your neck will get tighter and tighter and then let go and this will go on for months maybe even years as

you learn to be more present, so that your presence
alone will dissolve quicker the noise within you

This is the process, you don't know it is the process but it is is, a process that
you are unaware of until you reach that point that tipping point where you
realise that you are master its no longer an intellectual idea that you try to
grasp that you try to understand , somehow it becomes a realisation in you as
gurdjieff would say it is a crystallisation he would talk of points where you
would crystallise and this is one of those points a genuine life changing
tipping point in its own way really you would make cake and have a huge
celebration if we were that sort of society where we understood things of an
internal nature but of course we are not, it not only is it not celebrated
externally, but you may not really even fully understand it internally,
although this is one of those points at which it doesn't really happen until
you have the understanding and wisdom to know what has happened many

of the tipping points that you have had before this one will have happened and you will l not only have been unaware of them but even if you'd been aware of them you wouldn't of understood them, because you had not reached that point of understanding, now when reaching the tipping point that we will call the crystallisation of awareness you have the vantage point of hindsight and vantage point you are now looking back and understanding your meditational life up to now and also understanding much better the way in which you behaved in an unconscious way most of the time and in a way that you would much rather forget and find it difficult to forgive, realising now that you were unconscious almost all of the time so how could you blame yourself but still you do, to a greater or lesser extent and you will also look at others in a different way your subjectivity will have moved and you will see genuinely others in a more compassionate way because you've realise that they are almost totally unaware of their internal condition and the way in which they act out of that condition, if they have anger they have anger because they have pain, the list is endless, none of these things they are fully realised,

back to the legs look at effort, effort is one of those things that you may find you are pushing to its limit shall we say you can see some sort of light ahead and you are really going for it, you're meditating longer you are putting in a lot of effort this will be self defeating because effort is of the mind effort is born out of the idea that you can create something,this will work if you are building a business or making a cake but in meditation the more effort you exert the more pressure you will build up inside,effort is of the mind, so become aware of this effort, time after time just become aware of the push that you are exerting and it will fall away,

you may really be into the idea of enlightenment you may be a member of a group of Sanyasins or followers of a master and you really enjoy the pleasure that you get from this group or from the books from the idea of meditation and enlightenment and it will become a hobby, let me repeat that it will become a hobby and you will find it pleasurable, and you will store knowledge, and you will feel comfortable that you have more knowledge be aware of this you need to be aware that you may be more knowledgeable but you still have this sense of iness. so look within and address this time after time, if you look at the face from within you will see it most clearly there the face you are holding time and time again, lets go to the source of this as we look within the head area and rather than just dealing with how it feels, is it tight, is a unmoving is it in motion, this time we need to look at the front of the face and this is quite a difficult one to talk about and understand , but it is something that at this stage you may well have seen before and it is this face that you have, that you are holding so lets take it apart let's start with the mouth there is always a lot of tension and tightness and pain and emotion around the mouth there is the mouth that you show to the world and there is the mouth that you have within, some people have a real separation within this area they may be constantly smiling but underneath they are gurning and as you look closer and closer at this mouth area you will notice more and more tightness tension and pain and I,ness if you keep looking and feeling this area, imagine you are looking out on this face for the first time, you will gradually see what I mean it has a persona to it a flavour .

there is tremendous amount of work to be done on this face area every time you look in grasp it, be alert to it, just observe.

The home of the ego of course is in the head so if we are to master the head we must tackle two problems one is its constant chatter, and two is this sense of, I, now this I, when watched eventually is understood , it becomes an oh I see what you mean moment, you are observing the ego,

when you have softened the head neck and shoulders and you have energy within that area so that the area is no longer hard and unmoving you need fresh energy within that area, then this understanding really kicks in, if you have a stiff neck you won,t understand ego I,ness

I cannot stress this enough so not only do you need to soften the neck area but you also need to look into from behind so to speak, at your face I don't know really how to put it any other way it is such a difficult thing to talk about we have reached a stage where we are looking at subtleties and this is a subtlety that I can only describe as best as I can, so what I would say is you are looking at the back of your face and you need to realise that the way that you hold your face the way you always have done or in fact that's not quite true because the way you hold your face now will be a little bit different than when when you did when you were a child, you notice how if you feel hurt then your mouth puckers is a bit more or a lot more,(that's a good time to see it) and you are just that little bit more aware of your facial area in fact you are really quite aware of it and you can see what I mean, so bring your attention on to this face that you are wearing now and see if you can recognise it and feel it and just watch it and watch it and and watch it to death, the face is unconciouss firstly,and its there because that is who you think you are, but you are not that, you are the one that is observing that face not the one who has that face, there is a difference that becomes easier to understand with self separation, when the observer seperates from the observed ,or to put it another way, the ego slowly weakens and the witness,ing pure awareness becomes clearer, or to put it another way , when you observe yourself you are no longer right in there, being the noise you can observe the noise with more detachment,

And this self separation will speed up by your ability to work on this facial area to see the face as not yourself but something separate from yourself this may be confusing but this of course is great, confusion is something that you need in large doses sometimes you will be confused for weeks at a time and this is truly marvellous you need to celebrate again with a cake every time you are utterly confused it is a breakdown of the ego so looking at the back of the face the mouth the eyes will bring a new understanding to the dilemma of the ego until you separate from this face you will not understand the ego you may give it lip service you may think you understand it intellectually but really it is not the case until a certain level of self separation is reached and you are more awareness than you are face, This whole area will begin to soften along with the shoulders, over time until you reach a point where your neck and head and shoulders really give way and flow remember this area may have been stiff for tens of thousands of years I remember years ago when I really got to grips with my skull I had trigeminal neuralgia immediately afterwards, and for anyone who has ever experienced it you will know that it is no joke I can remember driving out in the car and screaming in agony this luckily didn't last for long I went in and softened up again and managed to overcome the problem fairly quickly but you will come across many painful areas in your body as you learn to face the present moment,

this really takes us on to the next issue which is this problem of just being still without there being too much pain, discomfort or pressure to bear.

It really needs to be understood that as you come close to being present in this moment your biggest problem is the amount of discomfort that you will face in your body, which will place a pressure on the mind to think, also physical pain at this stage in the game,

you can experiment with this, try it right now

be absolutely still in your head for one second after another, and keep this going one second at a time and you will soon discover that the pain and discomfort is much to bear, you will need to adjust your breath to cope with the discomfort that you feel in your body

When you reach this stage you are really at a turning point because you will understand that you simply cannot be still for very long without immense discomfort that you must overcome,(if you don,t feel discomfort then you are not still)

And this is this overcoming that we will look at next

this ability the strength that you need to face down the discomfort and pain, strange confusing sensations, and confusion itself, that you will feel as you reach the point where you can be still moment after moment after moment we could easily have put this section in the first stages because some of you may realise quite early on that this really is the crux of the matter can I sit and be still and why is it that when I do attempt this there is so much pain and discomfort in the body

you need to understand that if you don,t have the discomfort its not that you have,nt got any its that you are not realising that you are thinking

this problem really in a nutshell is what this book is all about is looking at this central problem of the discomfort and pressure that you will feel as you attempt stillness and how you can overcome this problem,

so with your eyes closed you have entered your head, so that you have a real grip of any thoughts that are there and this includes trying, or wanting,or wishing, or hoping you've seen all those problems so you simply wish to sit without thought, you are attentive to the sensations in your body and as you move into second after second of stillness you will feel a difficulty with breathing, so you will need to alter your breath and breathe your way through this stage,stuck emotion is stuck breath, in the same way that emotion and thought are entwined it is the same with emotion and breath,

any emotional buildup that you have especially in your belly will mean that breathing is difficult when the emotion goes in to the body initially your breath is disturbed reflecting the disturbance of the emotion, so as you face this emotional discomfort again you will feel the breath problem, sometimes your belly will lock up, so you need to take control of your breath so that you can make your way through this emotional turmoil that you feel,

you may have physical pain but hopefully by now you will have overcome many of the hard painful areas in your body by one way or another , with my back for instance it took me about 3 years to overcome the constant pain that I felt in my back whenever I sat to meditate and put any pressure on the moment,I did this by myself but I would advise you to get some assistance in the form of healing massage or any therapy that may help your meditation, so that it is not to painful when you sit and face the moment, it is very wearing to face pain time after time, it is nessasary to be internally tough but I cant see many people being as passionate about pain as I was,

this ability to face the moment is something that you may not have been able to do seriously up to this point, as you may not have been able to approach anywhere near empty, anywhere near silent, in your head, or empty enough in your body so that you can actually put pressure on the moment and hold yourself at that point of no thought,

adjust your breath so that you can make your way through it and just keep going for as many moments as you can, and each day when you feel that you are ready attempt this process, sometimes you can only do it once or twice a week you may feel that during the week in the evening you may have built up so much emotional nonsense during the day that you need to do the best you can, face it down and watch it, keep your body clear and then on the weekend when you have a little more time attempt this facing the moment, putting pressure on the moment like this being present being absolutely fully present moment after moment is a real milestone in your ability to overcome the body and move forward to the next step of really being able to master one moment after another and putting each moment together in a string of moments this may seem quite crazy that even after all these years you have only reached this point but remember only 45 min of stringing these moments together would give you enlightenment so even your first few seconds is a great step along the way because you start with a few seconds and then you can stretch that into a few minutes then clear or almost clear of thought again and again this sounds crazy just a few minutes without thought without motive free of discomfort is a great step along the way,

when you read autobiography of a yogi by yogananda there are many times where his master Shri pashwea chastises yogananda for not being silent enough to receive his mental messages, and many times whilst reading books by Masters and students you will find that the master will be chastising the student for not being still and present so it is something that we all must go through, if you are with a master then the master will be pushing you on, but in modern times where you may have only books by

Masters then you must be self-motivated, you don't understand the process
that a master, were he present, would be putting you through and the
master would be putting you through the process that he himself has been
through, and his master before him, so when you read the books of a
master you keep yourself close to the central core of the process, whereas
if you read books that are too fluffy you will find that you don't have a
masters understanding of things to fall back on, the reason that I have
written this book is because at the age of 57 I have spent most of my life
addressing this central issue of how do I become free of thought free of
ego free of discomfort and emotion able to obtain the master state which
isn't much to ask for really when you consider it, I just wish to be master
of this body I wish to be still, I wish to be free of the weakness of hurting
others so the central theme of this book the way in which this book can
help in a way that the master cant and I'm not suggesting that this book of
course can do more than a master but the way in which it can help is it can
help you to relate to someone who is going through the same problems in
the day to day way or someone who has been or is going through what you
are about to go through and talk about it in a mundane simple way because
often when you read the words of master they are so far ahead of us that
it is difficult to relate your life to theirs,whereas for instance in my case I
would consider myself as a budding master with L plates I have reached
the point where I know that I am the stillness that I can be still for
considerable periods at a time much easier than I could only a few years
ago but I am not at that point where I am still all of the time, but knowing
that I am that stillness means that I can no longer deny the fact that I am
the master state I am like a deputy headmaster who belongs to the
headmaster's union but most of the time still feels like a child and has days
where he totally cocks up and behaves like the ego he still has as a front
man , I also feel when I call myself a budding master with L plates that it
is wrong of me to do so, well it may be, but one of the things that you will
find on this trip is that you must all of the time experiment move forward

make mistakes that is what this path is all about you will constantly go astray but it is only in going astray that you realise that you have done so, but you are still a little bit further forward, so if it is a mistake(learning) to say that I am a master with L plates then so be it I must do so, because I cannot deny that now I realise or as gurdjieff would say it is crystallised in me that I am the stillness I am the awareness and not the noise I am not so identified with being the person as I used to be it has loosened its grip to some extent although it is still there this idea this ignorant concept that we have that we are the person and not the energy after all we have had this concept for tens of thousands years

putting your self under pressure

this moment to moment makes you more aware of this head belly issue and you will find that as you put yourself under pressure attempting to just be still it is your belly where you feel the discomfort the inability to breathe,the anxiety a slightly burning sensation,

you are watching the belly from the head area, but the sensation is in the belly this is an important thing to note because this is what will change over time, the observer will dissolve from its base in the head to be spatial leaving the belly sensation and sensation in general, as the head area dissolves even your notion of belly arm neck etc will not be there,because this body parts idea is from the head,

lets observe this head neck area closely in order to dissolve it observe the face that you are wearing the actual skull itself is pretty sensationless most of the time it hasn't got a lot of the easy to feel sensation to it as the belly has *but it is riddled with a foggy confusion that is very difficult to be aware of* you may be aware of course of the tightness in your neck rising up into your skull you may have quite a lot of tightness in your mouth and jaw, we need to talk about the eyes for a bit here I guess your eyes are quite interesting firstly they may be flickering and something that we haven't really looked at is this requirement to bring your eyes up to your third eye area and just lock into the third eye as opposed to being locked into your physical eyes bring your eyes up and gently see how the area in the centre of the forehead feels and it sort of becomes a little bit tingly , there will be some energy that will come to life, bringing the eyes gently up words and locking into your third eye means that you can see internally the third eye is really quite different from the physical eyes you might expect to see in through your inner eye in the same way that you see externally with your physical eyes but it's not like that, with your inner eye it is more a case of a cross between experiencing what you see, and what you see is more like an imaginary scene than an external image,although everones inner sight is different just as everyones external sight varies, let me recount the story that would give you an idea of what I mean many years ago I attended a workshop by a chappie from Hawaii and the workshop was called micro-movement bodywork and the chappie was telling us that the sensations that we felt as we were working on someone else were micro-movements of the body this was something that I totally disagreed with at the time as I could see quite clearly that it was energy that we were dealing with and not micro-movements of the tissue and this did not go down terribly well when I suggested this but I was younger then and less this diplomatic but I told the truth as I saw it and I would do the same again today but that is not the issue here that's just by the by, what i did experience very strongly was as I was working on someone I could see their body on the surface as tectonic plates as on the Earth's surface but as I could see this I could also feel it as well and it was as though what I could see I could also experience, this gives you an idea of what I mean, so when you actually see something with your inner eye and want todismiss it as nothing it will actually be your third eye but you may not recognise it as such, it can also be quite quick it can be there one moment and gone the next, something that we also need to look at whilst we are looking at the eyes is what I would call the problem of the itchy eyes and to explain this I need to go back to when I was an iridologist and noticed that when people

were emotionally charged the whites of their eyes would be bloodshot,
when I read the books they would suggest that this is because of inflamed
organs but this did not seem to be the whole story to me especially when
in later years I would suffer from itchy eyes if I was in the company of
other people, i later came to understand that the whites of the eye
correspond to our aura the Fibres of the iris correspond to the body and
the pupil corresponds to our centre like mysterious black holes in the
cosmos, when you meditate effectively sometimes you will find that you
will have very itchy eyes as the emotion in your body is broken down in
the same way as if you are mixing with people and you are affected by
there emotion you almost get hayfever from mixing with some people you
will also have symptoms of gas in the belly from their emotions you may
not notice it in short doses and even if you do you may give it some other
cause such as the food that you ate, but the more you understand your
body and its symptoms you will see that it is what you pick up from other
bodies as you become more sensitive more claresentient and to some
extent more fragile, on this problem of mixing with other people you will
also pick up ignorance from other minds which can at times be a little
disturbing as you will often find that you have much clarity and then you
move amongst people and find that your mind and your clarity is turned to
Mush and you worry that you have lost your understanding of things for
good, but don't worry again this is similar to emotional build up your
clarity will will return as you become still, sometimes when you look
within there is just a wall of foggy confusion,

*this confusion is the mental confusion happens as the ego dissolves< arises out of the body
especially the head neck*
*area it is a great way for the ego to stop you in your tracks when you get this fog you try
hard to understand and work your way through it this is exactly what you don,t want
to do as it prolongs the confusion and gives the ego what it wants if you starve it with
stillness clarity will be there quickly but it is also to be said that confusion is a wonderful
thing, in that it is a sign that your ego is breaking down*

over the years this will happen less often your body will become more and more transparent to the pure life force the intelegence that is below, your body will be less of a barrier less dense so the pure intelligence that's below will be more easily available because your body is filled with less emotion/ tension, discomfort, ignorance, mind, knowledge, and stagnation, stagnation I guess really is the word that for me best describes our human problem we have ponds of emotional stagnation in every corner of the body so that life, energy itself, cannot be felt cannot be understood because it cannot make its way through this wall of stagnation many years ago I was taking a course in London and we were treating a lady with arthritis and this lady was on the table and I really, really, had a strong desire to show everyone how arthritis is stagnant emotion and that it is the initial cause of arthritis but I wanted them to really understand it,to experience it so for that they really needed to feel it and so did the lady on the table, she had bad arthritis in just about every joint , so lying on the table with about 15-20 people the only way that I could see that I could show everyone and everyone could understand and feel the emotion was each person placed one finger there wasn't enough room for them all round the table one finger on the lady and I asked the lady herself if she would slowly move her attention from the tips of her fingers up through into her wrist her elbows and shoulders etc and then after this we did from the tips of her toes up through to the knees etc, and I asked everyone in the in the room including the lady on the bed if they could be 100% attentive to where her attention was and to feel the area within the body as the attention was slowly brought up through to the joints,and in a perfect combination of the atension and experiencing leading to understanding there wasn't a single person in the room who didn't feel the absolute complete grief that the woman had placed in the joints of her body, she would be sobbing her heart out when she reached the joint and then we would move on slowly through the limb to see if there was any more then reach another joint and again more sobbing and she went home free of pain, now some people would say I was even speaking to a lady only yesterday and I happened to mention that I'm a healer and it's not something I often talk about these days with normal people and her words were, 'yes I met someone one who believed he was a healer and I think that some of his healing even worked on my friend for a day but then of course the pain returned,

this is how people understand the healing arts(or don,t understand I should say) but then if the body is not understood then of course it is totally possible that the joints will again be filled with emotion, by understanding this problem the person with the arthritis will automatically be better able to help themselves as they understand that as they become emotional they need to address the problem in some way they need to see a healer they need to treat themselves with Bach flower remedies they need to sit with the crystal whatever they are able to do this is all a great help in the path towards eventually having a body free of emotion and discomfort it is not for everyone this path of facing down their own trials and tribulations this path of becoming a master it is in fact for very few but you can help others to some extent with their body problems one of the hardest tasks may be of a healer is realising how many people you can't help and in fact you can't even mention to many,

years ago I was surrounded by almost solely animal rights vegans and vegetarians and new-age thinkers and to talk freely about just about anything was something that I almost took for granted now for the last 14 years I mix with normal people who have no concept of energy life force vegetarianism at Or any such ideas and who much of the time can be openly hostile to such things especially in rural areas were hunting and cruelty is seen as the way of life,

so coming back to being fully present within the head we have noticed we are wearing a face, you cannot do anything about it,

you are you are just to notice these things just be aware of it, notice
very closely the movement of thought within the head we are just
talking about the thoughts you may have such as I wonder what I
will have four teatime but you will notice that there will be a much
subtler layer of things going on such as wanting to be still,or
anylising the body parts you must look for that and become aware
of it, it may sound silly to say such a thing because this is what we
are looking to achieve   this stillness but the wanting of it is a subtle
thought, we are to be present just present, free of the wanting and
free of the trying, any effort any trying needs to be dropped, and
this is why it's so difficult to use words to explain what to do
because the words will be used in an effort, and in trying, we need
to understand this understand this problem so you are not to try and
achieve stillness moreover you must observe the tryer the one who
is trying to achieve this is the one in the face the one who Wears
that face this is where it begins to not only be difficult to describe
but difficult to understand, what I am trying to describe being still
and present will not feel real, instinctively you will know that it is
not real if you are still trying,

And this is merely because there is still a doer someone who is
doing, you are still doing something as opposed to pulling back and just
watching you need to be very patient with yourself and persevere because
this stage will pass, to understand you're in your head your observing
whatever is there and you realise that you are still doing and you realise and
I repeat this again I know that somehow it is just not any different than its
always been your meditation is still the same and you don't know why but
instinctively you just know it's not the earth shattering experience that you

want, but this in part is due to the fact that you do want an experience, so that you can talk about it and feel that you are getting somewhere and also in part is due to the fact that the face that you are wearing the I, the I am, is still fully intact, and self separation although it will be in the process of happening is a slow process you will not be able to fully realise that you have pulled back, but you just don't realise it, so you need to be attentive to the two main issues, the face that you are wearing and the amount of stiffness and tightness in the body, of the neck shoulder area, until your shoulders neck and head have fresh soft energy it will be very difficult to understand the more subtle nature of I am, so slowly work on your shoulders and neck and at the same time be attentive to the face that you wear like a mask that's always been there, I know this is a problem to understand this face business, you are not doing anything wrong by not understanding what I mean, it is not that you have not read enough books you could read all of the books in the library and you would still not understand this face that personifies who you think you are, it is really an issue of identifying yourself as a person, assuming that you are a person so in other words you think that you are a person, someone who is a nurse or an electrician or a healer, you assume that what you think is part of who you are, you assume that the emotions that you feel are part of who you are, you assume that your opinions or your likes and dislikes, and all that you have knowledge of is who you are, but this is not the case this is what you have to dissolve so that you can realise you are the stillness that lies behind, so in other words the person that you think you are is just an acting front man, it's only on the surface it is based in the head, so what you are observing will slowly dissolve because it's not real, and you will be left with the Observer still peaceful, no wanting,wishing or trying, it is free of those things, slowly this notion that I am putting forward will become part of your being because you will experience it, as you read books by Masters they will be saying the same thing using different words and that's really the only valuable thing that I can do within this book is to use different words to describe the same process, and to describe the process in detail because for a master they have largely forgotten this preamble to enlightenment for them they have moved on to a much finer understanding and for them to ramble on as I do about this problem that you and I face would be difficult because that is not where they are at, they have moved on and they seem then to make it sound so simple, they say, do not think be still, and they don't talk too much about the difficulties of just achieving that, don't get me wrong they have been through it just as we are going through it now but they have reached the other side of the river and they are in a different place, for them it is still and they are looking back but for you and I we are still in the middle of the river paddling and so my aim with this book is to talk about the paddling itself what it's like inside the boat how we can paddle faster through the currents that we are in, and look at the beginning of our boat trip, the middle of the river, and as we reach the other shore, if there is anything that I wish to achieve with this book it is that,

so this this issue of the face observing it closely and talking about it and bringing it into the spotlight this is how we dissolve it this is how self separation works and if you place enough attention on the face mouth area you will begin to see it as separate from yourself in the beginning it is difficult to understand it is confusing what is he talking about, but keep watching and you will see there is actually what you would call a structure it has a real solidity to it this is how you feel about yourself this face and head that you have created within your life has become a real solid structure and has much emotion behind it, if you watch time after time and feel your way into the hardness you will find that the hardness will soften and you will feel the emotion that lies beneath, and even if you don't really understand what you are looking at because at this stage you are right up like saying the mind is watching the mind as opposed to saying awareness is watching the mind eventually as self separation runs its course it becomes much easier to observe this structure of the head because you have gained some distance from it but to gain that distance you must persevere with this early stage become fascinated by it, watch your mouth the way you hold it, and how it's not just the mouth the way you hold it is the way you have been hurt somehow, you don't need to analyse what the hurt was and why, if you analyze then the analysis is coming from the mind

so just observe as a silent witness

And slowly as months ago by you will loosen its grip you will most likely have a glimpse a gift of what it's like beyond the mind as you put pressure on this area it tends to crack an opening will appear and all of a sudden you will get a glimpse of yourself in a different perception, you will be observing this head area from beyond not within it and this gives you a great push it gives you momentum something to look forward to, it spurs you on but after it is gone a small piece of it will remain but you may not necessarily know it,

in other words you will never be quite the same again your ego perception will have shifted you will be in a different place but you may not know it, in fact it is most likely that you won,t this is so subtle within the body so very subtle that it is usually not spoken about it is left to the person to sort out themselves Krishnamurti said no one can teach you to meditate, you could say that what we are attempting with this book is this attempt at talking about describing the inner world so that at least we have some description of the process itself, what you are likely to find what you can expect and how to overcome, for me if I cannot at least try to assist in this inner process then I feel to some extent guilty as I feel that this is at least some way in which I can be of assistance to someone else starting out or going through the same process, I guess you know yourself that when you start a new job you feel so alone until you speak to someone else and you find that they went through the same process all of a sudden it makes it so much easier, you feel so much more at home in that new company to realise that everyone else went through the same as you,

so this is a major issue in this middle stage of the river bringing the awareness of the face,neck and shoulders,in to conscious,ness being conscious of the tension in your body means that you begin to understand what that tension is so that it will slowly fall away, likewise you are now watching a more subtle part of yourself, you are watching what you actually think you are, but are not, and this is confusing because it seems the mind is watching the mind but actually it is something more distant observing the mind it is pure awareness,and that's what you are, and pure awareness will become clearer as mind becomes still, it has just occurred to me at this point that some of you may be wondering why I haven't mentioned the higher self before and that is because my understanding of it is that that this is simply a Western concept that was picked up on some years ago and is still running you will never hear a master talk of the higher self it just confuses it's just one more concept among many, lets come back to this issue of being still for one moment and when you have this discomfort of breath which throws you off course you set out with the idea of just one moment without thought and another seems easy enough but when you really get to crunch point and you can really get your act together get inside of your head, silence it, and there is no subtle thought then what happens is that the belly begins to play you up your breath will go all over the place and throws you off course this is because because there is still emotion in the body which is disturbing the breath when the emotion went into the body it disturbed the breath and now when you face it again because you have come into the moment you will feel this disturbance again emotion and breath are intertwined, so when you face this breath disturbance firstly you know you're your right up against emotion that is stored in the body so make your way through the breath by taking control of it, however you find is right for you I know that for me I find that if I can break the breath and fall into the emotion without thought then it transforms it, the body tissue becomes soft,(in other words the tension on the surface) the belly will feel as though you have heart burn or indigestion as the emotion is dissolved , when you've made your way through this uncomfortable disturbed period it will be easier for you to be still in the future, there will be less turbulence in the belly and the belly will simply come to life, and it is your way of locking into the belly, as you locked into the third eye, locking into the belly is a very physical thing it's not something that you can ,think, of doing and this is why, for many years, because I was reading the books that you must move from the head to the belly but all the while that you, try,   because the tryer is the head, the head has more to do and is in its element, it is the very problem itself, the head is trying to open the belly, so it's a whole shift in understanding and perception, you understand firstly that your belly is disturbed and not working correctly, then you understand why,firstly because it has emotion in it, and you will also feel the disturbance from the rest of the body in it, also the other reason is because for many lifetimes the belly has not been in charge, has not been active at all, so you are bringing something to life that has been an unconscious dumping ground for so long,

 our mind has been in control since we moved out of the forest and into a mind made, man made, world, that becomes faster as each decade goes by, so this belly disturbance is a period that you need to go through so keep persevering place yourself in the line of fire as many times as you can buy bringing your mind to stillness and understanding as you learn experientially by facing stillness constantly as many times as you can and you will find that over the months and years it will become eventually much easier as your body is carrying much less emotion I guess there are some people out there are who have much less disturbance in the body than I do as logically we all have this disturbance, this emotional buildup, and ego to a greater or lesser extent, males often for instance have a more solidified ego than women but of course this is a generalisation as there are female men and male women we are all a big mix, in facing this belly area, firstly you have become still in your head and then the disturbance in the belly happens,(it is already there of course) so it is a good idea to then bring your attentiveness, your alertness to the belly itself, keeping attentiveness in the head as well as the belly, for in truth with awareness you can be aware of the whole body, the mind does not grasp this well, so bring your attentiveness to your belly and get hold of the breath, work at a level find out what's best for you break it a little give yourself some good deep breaths just work your way through, I often used to think that it was like I was thrown underwater and drowning and it would be a real panic whenever I faced stillness, work your way through keep going and eventually it will begin to subside and die down and you may even make your way right through to complete calmness, but it is likely that you may only attain relative ease in your body before you find that you are thrown out of this boiling pot with the pressure it creates to think, another reason for this pressure, when you attempt to be still and in the moment, is that when you actually achieve it, and you are still, you are also putting the ego under pressure the ego exists when the mind is in movement so if you are thinking you're fine, but as you come to this mental slow down and stop, the ego becomes fearful, so this panicky feeling is not only there in the body, but because you've brought the mind to a standstill the mind/ego itself simply has a pink fit it feels its own death because you brought it to Full stop so this is another reason for this meditational task of bringing everything to Full stop, it needs to be done over and over again so that the whole body becomes accustomed to it and learns to cope and overcome,

let's run through the body so that we can get an overall idea of what it's like what we have to deal with, if we firstly start with the head and this is always really the place to start because if your head is running riot then your attention will be all over the place so if you bring your attention to your head be aware of what's going on, bring your mind to stillness check out your face be aware of the person that is residing there as best you can by being as intensely aware as you can, is the mouth puckered, sometimes there can be a pressure in the eyes this is because sometimes when emotion comes up when you're watching an emotional program on the tv for instance and you really need to cry but you don't because you don't wish to be a wuss then emotion can backup and not be released as tears and so there can be pressure within and behind the eyes,

so you've got a grip of your head you,v checked it out for wanting and trying and other subtle low level thoughts such as analyzing, you are fully present as the Observer, we need to lock into the third eye area just gently with this, no straining just bring your eyeballs up until you feel this sort of almost physical sensational locking in, this if you like is switching from your external eyes to your inner vision bring it to life so that you can see where you're going in the dark so to speak, for some people the third eye is already up and running fully active, if you see colour when you meditate or if you're working on someone then is an indication that you have an active third eye, for others this may not be the case, I myself for instance am clairsentient so my belly tends to be my eyes, for clairvoyants then this is your active area you can see clearly , come back to the throat just linger in that throat area see what you can feel can you feel for instance the energy centre there, can you feel any emotion, very often ther is this kind of upset feeling this feeling of almost a lump in the throat that you get sometimes after you've had an argument or emotional upset, you may get this almost smoky lumpy feeling in the throat, very difficult to describe but that is often there, as you check out your throat do you see that where you feel any emotion from this throat area is in your belly, although you are observing your throat and that maybe tight etc in other words you will feel physical sensation there, the emotion can be felt in the belly, and this is the same throughout the body the emotion of the area is always felt in the belly, the beat of the energy centre here is really quite fast compared to the base centre and for many people it is an area that is dormant, in british culture for instance men taught not to voice there emotions in comparison to American men who talk about their emotions and the way they feel much more openly than in British society where there is a strong culture of stiff upper lip not saying how you feel this tends to have a deadening effect on the throat area, whenever I used to do a talk or run a course I would usually find my throat centre would be slow to get going, it was very difficult for me to start a talk my belly and my throat would not connect, it has been a similar experience with this book as I am using voice recognition software and after days of speaking into it is now flowing relatively easy,

so as we look at the body again we need to reiterate that one of the differences between normal man and a master is a Masters body is free of emotion and his mind is still they go together , it is so because he has done this work he has seen the problem faced it come to terms with it, the problem has dissolved before his gaze if a master sat with you and placed his gaze within your body as though it were his own then your disturbance would be made conscious through him and it would fall away that effectively is the way I work nowadays when I work with someone rather than hands-on as in the early days it is now the way it works for me I am merely an observer of the problem that you have within, so if for instance you have asthma then to a medical man or a therapist your asthma would be caused by the environment or other external causes but for me I would not know what the cause was and would not profess to know what the cause was until I simply feel it and become conscious of it and then the tightness that is in the lungs will be released the breath will be normalised no more asthma and in the case of asthma it is likely to be a relationship problem and it may not be husband and wife relationship necessarily it could be a problem with another member of family or even outside of the family but you could say it is the inability to get this emotion of the chest that will lead to the asthma I remember many years ago and I will keep this relatively simple as I do not wish the person to feel embarrassed by being in the book but I was sat on the lawn talking to someone and behind me this person was walking up to the house and the tightness within there chest was like a vice and they used an inhaler the emotion had made its way into the the bone of the ribs, which is by the way not too much of a problem if you are dealing with emotion in others it just takes a little bit longer to dissolve, because it's a denser area but it will still dissolve,coming back to the throat when we talk of the throat we are also talking of the neck of course and understanding that in the front we have the throat which feels this lumpy emotional pain and at the back we have an area of tension rising up from the shoulders with both the front and back it's an area that is filled with the emotional smoke that has arisen from lower in the body because that's what happens the emotion may start down in the belly or lower and rises like smoke until it reaches this constricted narrow part of the body the neck, so the back of the neck will feel tight the front will feel upset and lumpy and the back of the neck with muscles running up either side of the spine is an area that you could say is just one of the last areas to finally give in and be mastered in other words is always a difficult area everybody has this area as a difficulty and in the latter stages of meditation and mastering the body you will find that you can keep this nicely soft and flowing in the earlier stages of meditation you can keep it relatively slack you can avoid any spinal problems but you may not be able to crack it completely it will always be a little bit stiff mainly because or partly because you will still be up against a lot of emotion rattling about your body, this neck area also corresponds to the lower back they both go together so you will find that to crack this neck area you also have to understand and overcome the lower back which we'll get to later , back to the throat feel the area as deep as you can, if you just attend the area don,t turn away you will slowly open it up feel the upset recognise how it can be linked to the mouth,

The jaw
can be a real problem for some people it was for me
for many years I had a jaw that would crack very loudly, and even to eat I
used to have to open and close my mouth sometimes with my hand,

we used to hire out motor homes and we had a couple came to rent one
and I could see that she had a lot of emotion in her jaw and she said that
she couldn't sleep and had steroid injections   and that it was really
Painful so when I suggested that it was because she was storing
emotion she said to me that that is exactly what she had told her husband
the week before, so even though she had never come across healing before
she jumped at the idea and it was very successful and by the time she went
on holiday in the camper her jaw was back to the way it should be, they
became friends after this and used to come to meetings but the husband
when he first heard what I was saying in that first healing session about
emotion etc found himself and to use his words scared of what I was
saying and I have often found this that people are quite scared of this area
of understanding,

so we've looked in some depth at the front of the throat and the back of
the neck
muscles let's move down to the shoulders, if you look at them, I mean
feel them, if you stay there and feel them for very long you will find that
they are up around your ears and it's the only way I can describe it but they
are being held up, you are holding them up around your ears, and your
head you are pulling down, this is so common and once you have seen this
and become aware of what you are doing seen how you are holding
yourself then your body will slacken itself in this whole area because
you've become conscious of what was unconscious, the shoulders are very
prone to feeling the weight of the world and it literaly works that way if
you feel pressure from work or home all the things you have to do then
your shoulders will become tighter and tighter and more painful, the

responsibility that you feel will be stored in the shoulders, as you deal with the shoulders these will slacken, but you will find that they tend to get tighter and then slacken over and over again , as we

move down to the elbows these can suffer from a similar kind of situation to the shoulders as you place more responsibility on yourself so the elbows can begin to play up so bring your attention firstly through the bicep area just below the shoulders see what you have there you never

know what you're going to find, I,ll tell you a story of a problem that someone had in this area she was a lady that came to a course that I was running and she was I guess in her 70s and she had arthritis in the bone and muscle in this middle upper arm area which was unusual and when I touched this area I had quite a movement in the heart and said to her that somehow this arthritis was connected to her heart and as I said this she had a flashback and realised what the problem was, and said that a few years earlier she had lost her husband and when he was in the hospital bed she had put her arm over the top of those bars that run down the side of some hospital beds to hold his hand and kept her arm there for a long period of time because she didn't want to take her hand away from his, and this incident that she went through of nursing her husband by his bedside was locked into the tissue and the bone and the heart , I have had other

instances similar to this were events have been locked into the arms, so looking into this area of the arm bring it back to life, feel it in comparison with other areas it is quite a good way of checking out the

whole body this comparison from one part of the body to another is like having a reference point how does it compare with another part and you'll see that one part is softer feels really peaceful and sweet and comfortable whereas another part is hard uncomfortable or disturbed and it's a

really good way of seeing what you have in front of you, is it as soft is it as peaceful as this other area, comparison infers a mental analysis and in the beginning it will be but eventually it becomes a feeling an awareness

If one area is in comparison to another it gives you reference points that you
can use to your advantage it is easy to check out an area of the body
and not really see it clearly feel it clearly but when you refer it to another
it becomes clear that it is much tighter than the other area, or it has
emotion in it that you didn't really feel whereas
the other area is peaceful this area feels somehow unpeaceful in
comparison, so now let's move down to the elbows and check them out in
the same way, the bones in the elbows are very much like the shoulders
they can suffer in the same way it seems to me the emotional content
required to do damage is this work load pressure feeling, in the elbows it
can also
be related to love issues for instance I knew of a lady who really did not get
on with her husband and used to come for healing when she could no
longer change gear on the car and it was because she had pulled back so
much from her hands the energy pulled back so far that her elbows were
almost locked and severely painful, in the beginning of a relationship when
you hold hands your energy comes out through your arms and meets the
other person and there is a lovely strong flow of energy coming out
through the hands no blockages always keeping the arms flowing and soft
and washing the emotion through, whereas if a relationship reaches the
point where you no longer hold hands and you no longer even wish to
touch the other then the arms become stagnant and the energy and blood
doesn't
flow and you will have pain I also remember a case that I had I was
running a course with a chap which was something that I'd never done
before he was very intent on running the course to a timetable and
itinerary which was and still is something that I couldn't even attempt and
would not wish to and I remember around mid-afternoon I think it was
when we had an itinerary of areas of the body that had to be done at
certain times can you believe, totally bonkers but never mind ,

I had a lady who we saw was in a dungeon and pulled herself up on her
elbows   and this was causing her what she and the
doctor called arthritis, so needless to say the itinerary went out the
window which did not go down too well but it had to be done until the
elbows were soft and let me explain soft for a minute if you place your
hand on someone else's elbow one on the bottom and one on top side
if you can feel flesh and bone between your hands then they are relatively
hard and sometimes they are so hard that they can be quite cold and hard
and this applies to any part of the body but I,m just trying to
explain softness in this way so if you feel flesh and it is quite solid and even
cold this is what I call hard and it is all a matter of degree, soft is when
there is nothing no elbow no flesh no blood in between so with your eyes
closed there is absolutely nothing in between your hands except the feeling
of energy and in this lady's case as in any one else when there is only
energy the job is done and she would have had no problems with those
elbows again from that past event,another incident that shows quite clearly
the effect emotion can have on the elbows was many years ago my partner
Was in intensive care and I had an animal sanctuary to run and a house
renovation in progress and other things as well at the same time and so I
was spending large amounts of time driving from house-to-house trying to
keep each one going as well as going to the hospital and the effect of this
was that each time I got into the pickup my elbow would almost instantly
give me excruciating pain and I would have to drive one-handed with the
other one resting in my lap whilst I drove for seemingly hours in agony I
did not worry about this because I knew what the problem was and that it
would go as soon as the stress was over and it duly did, moving down to
the forearms this is the area of carpal tunnel so check out how does it feel
inside very often this area of the arm is quite unconscious so you may
need to spend quite some time there to see how it feels is it rigid how is
it in comparison to other parts of the body this forearm area can be an
area that suffers from a feeling of being overworked hence carpal tunnel

itself is associated with using it in work repetitively but if this part of the arm is soft and flowing and the and emotion isn't there then repetitiveness will not be a problem, moving down to the wrist it is like the elbows and shoulders an area for arthritis this whole hand area can be an arthritis area it is the end of the body so if energy is not flowing through it both in and out then it is an area where emotion can stagnate so check out the hands can you feel the energy and because they are used so much they have a reasonable amount of sensitivity but still they can be quite unconscious especially the fingers they can store quite a bit unconsciously so bring them to life let's move on to the chest area and behind that of course is the back and the spine we'll deal with both areas separately as both have different emotions that affect them firstly the front as I said before this tends to be an area that is affected by relationship a build up of emotion based around relationships it can also be an area of anxiety we are often told that we should be breathing from the chest from the lungs but really we are better off breathing from the belly from lower down as this chest area is quite shallow and an area of anxiousness and although the lungs are there if you observe a child when he enters life he is breathing lower down we start in life with our breath low in the body and then as we get older the breath becomes so shallow that it is only just in the throat itself not even in the chest, as we look into this area check it out you will usually find that it is filled with this light anxiousness lightly disturbing your mind keep your attention there, dissolve it breathe into it then throw your breath out breathe in and throw out, keep this going so that you empty this area of this anxiety keep throwing out, this anxiety of course is slowly permeating through into the muscles of the back so as you look into the back you'll see that the front part of the chest is relatively un solid and more moving and flowing and fluffy feeling than the the back this area can be rigid unmoving stiff and unflowing filled with a much denser feeling a more depressive feeling in fact you may not feel the emotion of it at all as it is so dense, as you look into it if you can breathe in stretch and stretch and stretch and the front part the lungs the chest going into the back expand and expand your breath so that it moves energy into this back part and bring it to life make it as soft and flowing as the front part and you will not suffer from back problems, from the age of 16 to around my late-20s I suffered tremendously from back problems and didn't realise at the time it was because of this unflowing the amount I was storing in the back, the back is so long there is so much to go tight and the spine is in the middle if the muscles either side of the spine go tight they don't always do this in a uniform fashion of course one side may be much tighter than the other then this will put tremendous strain on the discs the spine itself and you will always be going to a chiropractor or an osteopath and as soon as they have put your back in line it will be out again, so you must if you want to be free of the burden of back pain you must clear this area get it soft and flowing and this does include this lower back area the line around the hips this beltline is very much responsible for much of the emotion that is in this back area oshos kundalini meditation is very good for softening the back as you just allow the body to make any movements it needs and this often has the effect of just unlocking the back even with the mildest softest movements I remember when I first started to use it I was swaying very very slowly and softly and not very long but the effect was tremendous my whole body became much softer when you see a child a young baby move they will make these movements these movements with the body that the energy wishes the body to follow and this is really the underlying factor with kundalini from the lower back take the middle back this area behind the belly this of course as you can imagine is affected by the fact that the anxiety that you feel may well be down around that belly area and this will make its way back through from the front to the back it may also be rising up from the lower back as we just said from the beltline this beltline is an area for resentment and some of the more base emotions such as fear and anger come out of this base centre as well as a general overall feeling of drudgery and despair will stagnate around this lower back and into the hips buttocks classic arthritis of the hips, plenty of physical movements physical exercise within that area will help to keep it flowing but of course you need to take care of the underlying problems within , rose quartz will help, some of the Bach flower remedies and again a good

technique is to push the breath right, right,down into this lower back push the breath in, breathing in and expand expand and expand into this area then let the breath fallout do this many times expand the breath, then fallout expand contract expand contract do it over and over and over again and experiment with breaking the breath in this area as well break the breath , break the breath with no rhythm or order to it ,like a sob, and you will break up the emotion in this area this broken breath technique that I mentioned in the first stage which is having a breath with no pattern to it will work really well in this lower back area it is one of the few things that will really get it moving it is such a solid stagnant area for so many people and is difficult to break open So don't be afraid to experiment with the breath, break your breath whilst you are attentive looking into it and you will also find that as you break this breath you'll also find that you will break open areas of actual pain you will have pain in your spine or in your muscles really so painful that you almost can,t go on but have a break and come back to it later and you'll find that the energy itself has continued to work and it has softened a little bit more go back to it, break the breath throw out and keep this up until you're back really feels alive and almost throbbing with energy and then you will be able to feel the energy centres in fact this is the point at which you will open a new chapter as when your body is soft and free of disturbance your energy centres will be ble to be felt , exercise fast exercise is really good there used to be many years ago a shamanic dance fast and flowing great it was a very circular dance all circles,it was all the rage in new age circles, bouncing up and down hitting the ground with the heels has the effect of opening up the energy in the spine this is why children stamp because instinctively they just doing what makes them feel better they stamp their feet releasing the emotion and energy up through the body opening up the energy centres bringing the body back to life again don't be afraid to experiment play with the breath expanding contracting I cannot stress this enough expand and contract your physical body much more so than you would ordinarily , so many times when I do this with people and I try to get them to really push their belly really push there back out they do it in quite a feeble way possibly because they are embarrassed but it is usually not in a way that is sufficient to bring about a good result be quite hard with yourself quite tough with yourself , really push your front as you breathe in really push your back expand your back as you breathe in and then the whole central section as you breathe out throw your breath out and start again until you feel that you have this really alive feeling you'll see that you can feel much more you may get a burning sensation in your stomach as the solar plexus centre comes to life you'll feel this almost like a burn or indigestion that you need to take antacids but that is simply because you've brought the stomach area to life, you will also get this as emotion is dissolved in the stomach area in the same way that food is dissolved, you will also find as emotion is released out of the body you could get cystitis, you may also get diarrhoea which is also again making its way out of the body one of my patients many years ago was a really good herbalist she was a Chinese herbalist and a british herbalist and she had done training in China and also in ceylon which now has a different name for the life of me I can,t think what it is but we used to go to a local meeting of therapists and she was one of the ladies there are and I remember I treated her belly area as I noticed that there was much fear there and the following month when we met again she said to me,as a herbalist I have tried every herb known to man but I have never in all my years had a solid stool they are very much into their stools the old herbalists this cracked me up and I said this was because we dissolved the fear : in speaking of this lady it also reminds me of an incident with her back in fact we were looking on this occasion at the fact that she had been in an accident and I believe from memory it was a car accident and she kept on putting her back out ,there was a therapists couch there so I said lay on the couch let's take a shufty and as I placed my hand over the spine I felt tremendous fear coming from one particular area one particular piece of the spine so I said well the first thing I need to do is just dissolve this fear here a minute because it is placing too much pressure on the surrounding area and is becoming brittle and inflamed and as I did this another therapist who was quite forceful kind of guy and was very sure of his own abilities in manipulating the spine more or less pushed me to one side and said you are working in the wrong area and being much younger and being affected by the fear that was coming out of the spine itself I more or less moved to one side and let him get on with it but this shows the difference in the way that people work and the way in which the accident itself for me was not so much about the physical problem that it had created but the fear that was trapped in the bone and although the therapist may well put the the disc back in given 2 min it will be back out again and it will not resolve the underlying issue, so coming back to the belt area let's work our way down to the hips, the hips themselves are really quite interesting because they are on this line of separation between the upper body and lower body its very much a problem for those who overwork people who overwork who don't have enough playtime and for those who worry about finances and very often both go together you overwork because you are worried about finances its quite normal for dairy farmers for instance where I used to live on the south coast in Dorset quite normal for many dairy farmers to have hip problems and they tend to blame it on the wet weather but dairy farming is such that you are up at five and you don't finish milking till 7- 8pm   and relief milkers cost money so they would be milking maybe seven days a week as well as doing all of the jobs around the farm so this tended to have a very bad effect on the hips because the feeling of being overworked overwhelmed by the the amount that you have to do, the feeling that you get when you first wake up and remember what you have to cope with during that day, that feeling of dread, dread being I guess the operative word this really does affect the lower back and hips and there is no way that you will sort this problem out unless you take care of the cause you're working too hard, working too long and not resting enough, another story of someone I know, it was when I started to notice that if I place my attention on someone then I will feel there symptoms, but in this case it was when I began to notice that the opposite is also true when they place their attention on me then I will also feel their symptoms, I was living on the south coast and somebody was coming that day from the North Coast so they were driving approximately 2 1/2 hours to get to me and I didn't really know what the problem was I had briefly met them at a course that I'd run that they came along to but I couldn't really remember what the issues were and I remember about 10 o'clock that morning and I they were due to arrive around 12 midday and I remember around 10 o'clock I was using a chainsaw cutting logs and I began to notice that my hips were starting to get more and more painful it started out quite mild and then it got to the point where I could hardly move and was hobbling with pain and I pretty much realised that it must be this person that was on their way to see me and by the time they arrived from memory she came down the drive to meet me and i told the story and suggested that the work had already been done and that we might as well just have a cup of tea and she could head home I said this jokingly but to some extent it was the case I had recognised and been made conscious of the fact that this was her problem and I knew that because I could feel it and become conscious of it her arthritis would soften and become much better she was quite a serious case and from memory she did get better because I see her now and again but I seem to remember that she would have needed from hindsight I would say 4 to 5 treatments at least an hour a piece and I got a feeling that she only came the once and I think it was mainly because of the distance that travelling distance was so difficult for her so when you look into your hip area and I include the buttocks in this area if you are one of those people who when you sit on a wooden chair you get bum ache this is an indication that you have not got enough energy moving in this area, the base centre suffers from the strong emotions here and it can tend to stagnate all through this hip lower back so as you become acquainted with your body you will feel that this hip area is quite a solid unflowing unmoving area so move into it spend quite a bit of time opening it breath into it again and again as you did higher up it may sound strange but you can breathe into the area as you could breathe life into pretty much any part of your body push your breath right down into the hips right down into that lower torso pushing and expanding push it right down again and again and throw the breath out throw out the stale emotion from this area breathe in and out continuously until again this this hip area comes to life as you did with the back, now lets move down into the the area above the knees between the knees and the hips bring that to life check it out see how it feels once this is done move down to the knees to see how they feel as I said before the knees tend to suffer when you have money worries, supporting yourself, they also suffer from past fight or flight situations if you have a situation of fear or anxiety which you would love to run away from but you have to stand and face it even if it is not a physical situation but maybe a confrontational situation or somebody that you have to work with, where does anxiety end and fear begin, because this is a hard bony area if you have pain here you may well need to see a healer so that they can soften this as it would take you quite a while before you can do it yourself, and this applies to any bony problem it may be easier to get help from a healer until you have a good precense, moving down to the shins and the calf muscles this is a great area to treat by placing your feet down into the ground remember in the beginning this will be imagination but eventually you realise that you are energy itself so imagination slowly moves into actually moving into the ground as energy by placing your attention on something you move into it that's what happens when you are looking into a house for ghosts or when you are going to buy a house you place your attention into the house as you look around and you realise there is a feeling there ,your attention takes you in so feel your way down into the ground and you will feel this tingling sensation of the energy slowly rising up your legs and if your knees are not blocked then you'll feel it rise right up through the body this is a great way to soften those knees should they be blocked as the energy comes up if you have blocked knees bring 100% of your attention into them so that you can bring them to life, down to the ankles and feet again dropping these into the ground is the very best way to deal with any ankle and foot problems this area will be affected by financial worries that you may have you'll find sometimes that if you worry about bills you just get this kind of pain in the ankle that will be there 1 min and gone the next I'm sure many people in the past have gone to the doctor with this problem and have been sent away maybe with anti-inflammatory, if the heel of the foot is hard on the ground and maybe painful this indicates low energy   again bring the energy up from the ground

And rest and you will find your heels become soft as your energy levels rise and they will merge with the ground so that you cannot

feel where your feet end and the ground begins,

The Later stage of meditation

this later stage of meditation I guess could be defined when there is that turning point in your internal world when you realise that you ,really are, pure awareness up to this point you have read it so many times that it has really truthfully been an intellectual belief but all of a sudden out of the blue something shifts inside and you realise that it is up to you as the master to keep yourself free of emotion and unwanted thought, of course in the beginning you will not be able to hold this stillness all the time but it is easier to hold it more of the time,something has changed internally, before this stage meditation was something that you did as often as you could to the best of your ability, now it is no longer meditation, you can rest in stillness because it is your nature to do so, the perception of what you are has taken a shift you are now more stillness then you are noise, before you were more noise than you were stillness when you become still the ego still squirms still trys to play you like an instrument but it is not the extreme discomfort that you felt in the middle stages,now it is not so much that you work hard to achieve stillness now stillness is there waiting to be recognized everything concerning meditativness is subtle, your energy centres will very quickly come to life when you are present it becomes much quicker and easier to dissolve the emotion as it settles from the day as you know that emotion is Not you and when that emotion creates a face and your mouth puckers it will quickly dissolve because you no longer so closely identify with it you will of course still identify yourself to a greater or lesser degree as a person thousands of years of miss identification is not going to fall away overnight, (until it goes in a second that is when enlightenment happens,) but due to self separation,and your ability to contain emotion, (this method that we have been looking at in this book is called the containment method,) becomes much easier no longer do you suffer in the way that you did in the earlier stages as you contain the emotion that you feel and it will fall much quicker and easier as your ability to be present grows stronger you can at this stage most likely bring your awareness onto any of your energy centres and as you do you'll feel

the area is soft and there is a soft beat, in this later stage the gross parts of
your body the hard physical painful tension type problems in your body have
been dissolved your ability to be present and a presence and your
understanding of this and bring about change relatively quickly now when you
get to this stage you are into even more subtle areas such as experiencing your
body as sensational you don't see it as much as my arm my neck, you don't try
any more or as much the learning process as you go along becomes more and
more subtle as you go along,

if a cat is looking at the clouds it just happens to gaze in that direction if a
weatherman is looking at the clouds then he is naming them he is predicting is
looking at the past where they've come from how they were formed what
they've got in them his self image is as a weatherman and wether he is good at
it etc so his gaze leads to lots of mental chatter, if you have a dial and the cat
is to the right and a weatherman is to the left as you look within now you have
moved the dial from left over to the right as you gaze within your eyes are
more like that of the cat than when you started as a weatherman, your ability
now to move from the head to the belly is much easier, partly because there is
no trying involved, your stillness is in your belly, you are less heady, you've
seen that you were based in the head most of the time, now you realise that
the task is to keep that belly as a centre rather than the head, as osho puts it
feel the centre and don,t for a second loose it , so it's a sensational feeling
thing you can't keep the centre alive by thinking about keeping the centre alive
it becomes your new centre it has a real beat it changes all the time deepens
and softens keeping the centre of the body softer and more flowy, so you have
now achieved from the early stages when the body was tense, tight, and
painful filled with decades and lifetimes of pain you have now moved to a
situation where the body is quite empty much less tense even the neck and
shoulders and into the head will now stay soft for most of the time you may
pick up some daily emotion of course you will still get emotional you will still
be affected by it but your ability to gain some distance from it has increased
and your ability to dissolve it quicker as it hits the body has increased in short

you have much more understanding and are more master of this body that you occupy for a while than you were before, the difference between the master and

the student is that of understanding. And alertness

Lightning Source UK Ltd.
Milton Keynes UK
UKHW020951201121
394268UK00010B/2420